Donald MacKenzie and The Murder Room

>>> This title is part of The Murder Room, our series dedicated to making available out-of-print or hard-to-find titles by classic crime writers.

Crime fiction has always held up a mirror to society. The Victorians were fascinated by sensational murder and the emerging science of detection; now we are obsessed with the forensic detail of violent death. And no other genre has so captivated and enthralled readers.

Vast troves of classic crime writing have for a long time been unavailable to all but the most dedicated frequenters of second-hand bookshops. The advent of digital publishing means that we are now able to bring you the backlists of a huge range of titles by classic and contemporary crime writers, some of which have been out of print for decades.

From the genteel amateur private eyes of the Golden Age and the femmes fatales of pulp fiction, to the morally ambiguous hard-boiled detectives of mid twentieth-century America and their descendants who walk our twenty-first century streets, The Murder Room has it all. **>>>**

The Murder Room
Where Criminal Minds Meet

themurderroom.com

Donald MacKenzie 1908–1994

Donald MacKenzie was born in Ontario, Canada, and educated in England, Canada and Switzerland. For twenty-five years MacKenzie lived by crime in many countries. 'I went to jail,' he wrote, 'if not with depressing regularity, too often for my liking.' His last sentences were five years in the United States and three years in England, running consecutively. He began writing and selling stories when in American jail. 'I try to do exactly as I like as often as possible and I don't think I'm either psychopathic, a wayward boy, a problem of our time, a charming rogue. Or ever was.'

He had a wife, Estrela, and a daughter, and they divided their time between England, Portugal, Spain and Austria.

Henry Chalice

Salute from a Dead Man
Death Is a Friend
Sleep Is for the Rich

John Raven

Zalenski's Percentage
Raven in Flight
Raven and the Kamikaze
Raven and the Ratcatcher
Raven After Dark
Raven Settles a Score
Raven and the Paperhangers

Raven's Revenge
Raven's Longest Night
Raven's Shadow
Nobody Here By That Name
A Savage State of Grace
By Any Illegal Means
The Eyes of the Goat
The Sixth Deadly Sin
Loose Cannon

Standalone novels

Nowhere to Go
The Juryman
The Scent of Danger
Dangerous Silence
Knife Edge
The Genial Stranger
Double Exposure
The Lonely Side of the River
Cool Sleeps Balaban
Dead Straight
Three Minus Two
Night Boat from Puerto Vedra
The Kyle Contract
Postscript to a Dead Letter
The Spreewald Collection
Deep, Dark and Dead
Last of the Boatriders

Knife Edge

Donald MacKenzie

An Orion book

Copyright © The Estate of Donald MacKenzie 1961

The right of Donald MacKenzie to be identified as the author of this work has been asserted in accordance with the Copyright, Designs and Patents Act 1988.

This edition published by
The Orion Publishing Group Ltd
Orion House
5 Upper St Martin's Lane
London WC2H 9EA

An Hachette UK company
A CIP catalogue record for this book is available from the British Library

ISBN 978 1 4719 0567 4

www.orionbooks.co.uk

For Richard and Monika Schulze-Kossens

NEIL MACFARLANE climbed on the barstool. He sat, folding the last *mille* bill lengthways, over and over again. Twice the waiter was forced to repeat his query before MacFarlane pushed the flimsy spill across the counter and ordered. He drank, staring into the mirror, holding the shallow glass with both hands.

Behind him the low-hung lamp over the green table caught the brilliance of a jewel, the fat curl of cigar smoke, as the players rose to their feet. Anyone leaving the *salle des jeux* had to pass him. First to come were the two Greeks, squat and Mayan of countenance. The elder as always a precise two paces in front of the other. The tall stooped Parisian banker, solicitous as he settled lavender mink round the young girl's shoulders.

Then the couple from MacFarlane's hotel. The man straw-haired, his well-cut tailcoat a foil for the woman's simple elegance. She moved with the grace MacFarlane had noticed a dozen times — her easy carriage and walk almost professional. Without turning his head, he knew they were

1

coming to the bar. Her scent was sharp as she passed behind him. The couple stood a few feet away. The man ordered drinks, his voice quiet and very English.

Conscious of the woman's appraisal, MacFarlane kept his gaze in the mirror steady. The Whitakers were the last to leave the table. Only the taut brown skin about MacFarlane's eyes betrayed his effort to show composure. He turned slowly on the stool, leaning his elbows on the bar behind him. By the time the Whitakers reached him, he was smiling. He slid from his seat to bend over Sarah Whitaker's hand. Ease of manner robbed the gesture of affectation.

He straightened up to meet her husband's broad smile. "Goodnight, Sarah! Goodnight, George!"

"That makes three times in a row that I've cooked your goose, Neil!" Childish delight sounded in Whitaker's voice. He started a laugh deep in his plump face, held it till it exhausted itself under the buttons of his white dinner jacket. Caught by some secret pleasure, his rotund middle started to work again.

His wife's voice was impatient. She shrugged still-good shoulders into her dark cape, wide-eyed with sympathy. "I wish you wouldn't be such a brat, George! Neil — I've never seen such wretched luck!"

"It goes like that." Holding this insane grin made his jaw muscles ache. Gas from the wine he had drunk troubled his nasal passages.

She touched his sleeve, the heavy diamond bracelet sliding the length of her forearm. "You can have your revenge on Thursday. We're seeing you, aren't we — eightish for drinks. I don't know that I can promise you any pretty

2

women. That shouldn't bother you as long as the play is good." Her voice was both coy and anxious.

"That's right — just the play." He still held the smile. Anything she was looking for, he would promise.

She smiled pleasantly. "We'll send the car about seven."

He stood courteously until they had vanished down the mirror-flanked corridor. The very rich, he thought sourly. A short six months ago he would have broken a leg for the chance to gamble with the Whitaker crowd. With somebody whose pitch lakes provided him with twenty thousand dollars a week — just as long as the man kept breathing. Whitaker didn't even need the luck he had — yet three cheap wins made him crow like a dunghill rooster.

Thought of the coming Thursday gave MacFarlane a gambler's inner assurance. It would be payday. Up at the Whitakers' house there'd be no Greek syndicate to buck — no inspired competition. Only the rich.

He said a mechanical goodnight to the barman. As he left his stool, he noticed the Englishman's frank stare. He waited for one defiant second, ready to lower the boom on a stranger's sympathy. Then pocketing his change, he made his way out of the casino.

A late September moon was on its back in the soft night. On the far side of the Croisette, white villas rose from walled gardens, improbable as birthday-cake decorations. Cap in hand, the chasseur was shutting the door of the Whitaker Rolls. MacFarlane waited behind a pillar till the car's taillights rounded the point.

An hour's drive, he thought, and they'd be high in the mountains beyond Grasse. Home in the stone-built manor house, the five hundred acres of pine and parkland — cool even in the furnace of a Mediterranean summer. It was no more than one of the four houses the Whitakers called home. He lit a cigarette, acid with frustration. There was no law against having that kind of money. To be eligible for gemütlichkeit you didn't have to live in a shack dripping with wetwash and owned by the finance company.

He was walking quickly, indifferent to the deep patches of shadow around the villa gates. The newspapers had been full of reports recently — late-night drunks robbed on their way home from the casino. It didn't matter. The Algerians would have small pickings with him. Prompted by the thought, he stopped — unstrapped the gold wristwatch and fastened it round his ankle. It would be hidden and it was always worth another pawn ticket. With Thursday two days away, he still had to worry about eating. As far as he knew, his credit in Cannes wasn't good for as much as a hamburger.

He rounded the curve into the hotel forecourt, stepping aside to let the white Jaguar convertible pass him. The floodlights came on and he saw the Englishman from the casino at the wheel. Tossing his car keys at the chasseur, the man walked his companion to a table on the terrace.

The hotel lobby was bright and unfriendly through the swing doors. MacFarlane put his weight on the heavy glass. The sound of the revolving door brought the night porter to his feet. His sallow face lost expectancy as he recognized MacFarlane. He dropped back on his seat and picked his teeth with passion.

MacFarlane kept his hands steady on the polished wood in front of him. His voice was tired. "Four-three-seven, please!"

The porter groped in the niches behind, his eyes never leaving MacFarlane's face. Pulling out a pale blue envelope, he held it aloft for a moment, poised between thumb and forefinger. It dropped on the counter.

"For you, monsieur!"

MacFarlane broke open the envelope. He read the bill's total automatically. "Four-three-seven," he repeated.

The porter was rocking slightly on his stool. He folded both arms across his chest, shaking his head. "My instructions are that Monsieur would be good enough to settle this bill tonight!" He made no secret of his personal skepticism.

MacFarlane pushed his hands deep in his jacket pocket. The man was near enough to be grabbed by the braided lapels — shaken till respect replaced the sneer on his face.

"I'll take care of it in the morning. Right now I'll have the doorkey."

The porter made no move. To the right of the desk a light shone through a glass panel marked MANAGER. MacFarlane spoke on impulse.

"Get the night manager — I'll talk to him!"

The porters' eyes were wary. "I am sorry, monsieur. Monsieur Peugeot is not to be disturbed."

The few steps MacFarlane took carried him no more than feet from the manager's office. "Either you'll get him or I will!"

The porter shuffled towards the lighted door, muttering. Outside the entrance loomed the white-capped chasseur, his curiosity beyond control. Indifferent to the man's regard, MacFarlane reached behind the counter and took his doorkey. The office door opened. Somber-clad, his bearing that of a cleric interrupted at a funeral, the manager followed

the porter to the foyer. He inspected the length of Mac-
Farlane's body before speaking.

"You wished to see me, monsieur?"

"I do. This bill . . . I'll take care of it in the morning."
He pushed a finger in the direction of the porter. "There's
another thing — I'd like you to see that this individual gets
a lesson in common courtesy."

Peugeot's eyes grew glassier. "I regret that you should
find cause for complaint, monsieur. Still more since this is
a case of a man doing his duty." He made himself a little
taller. "*I* gave the instructions that your bill should be paid
tonight. The porter has no authority to vary them." He finished smugly. "Nor have I since they are those of the
managing director himself. Your bill, monsieur, is two
weeks overdue."

"What of it? You're not suggesting that I'm going to skip
without paying, are you?" MacFarlane caught his stam-
mer. He raised both hands, looking down ruefully at white
jacket, thin dress trousers and evening shoes. "Am I supposed to walk the streets of Cannes till the banks open,
dressed like this?" The manager's eyes wavered. "I could
always go to the police," MacFarlane said casually. "Tell
them I'm locked out. I hardly think it would be pleasant
for either of us."

Peugeot's mouth was adamant. He spread his shoulders.
"You are a man of the world, monsieur. And I think we
understand one another. To go to the police is your right —
I hardly suppose you will exercise it. Now if you will excuse
me!" He bowed from the neck and went to his office.

The porter slumped, hiding his grin behind his newspaper. The straightbacked chair across the hall was a refuge.

6

MacFarlane sat down, lighting a cigarette with shaking hand. The management would want no scandal in a place of this kind. Certainly they wouldn't go as far as man-handling him from the premises. He'd give it five minutes then sneak upstairs. Later he'd have to get his bags out somehow — with or without paying the bill. He looked across the lobby.

The house detective had joined the group at the desk. Hard-eyed and with his dinner jacket buttoned in haste over a pajama top. None of the three men was watching MacFarlane. Keeping close to the edge of the wall, he walked to the bottom of the stairs. Once he felt the deep carpet underfoot, he started up on the run. Dim lights burned in the corridor. A white-aproned bootblack passed him, incurious, his arms full of shoes.

Whistling softly through his teeth, MacFarlane turned his doorkey. Nothing happened. He took the key out and tried again. The door still held. Lifting his head, he saw the small steel padlock high on the doorjamb. Thin white cord followed the line of the hasp, finishing in a clot of sealing wax. The whole effect was official and somehow sinis-ter. Possibly the management had already informed the po-lice. A cistern flushed noisily down the corridor. He started, expecting to see the house detective appear. After listening for a few seconds, he made his way down, feet dragging a little. He passed the silent group at the desk and went out to the terrace.

All but four of the tables had been stacked for the night. A few chairs were left by the fountain. The Englishman and his companion were sitting a few feet away. Conscious of their raised heads, MacFarlane took the table next to them.

The solitary waiter came over, hollow-faced with fatigue.

"Champagne — a bottle!" MacFarlane gave a brand name and year. He shut his eyes, leaning his head against the swing seat. The woman's murmur was too low for him to distinguish more than an occasional word in accented English. He looked up, hearing the chink of metal. The waiter was spinning the bottle of wine in its bucket. He wiped his hand on his napkin and gave MacFarlane the bill.

MacFarlane's pen speared the paper as he scrawled his signature. He added his room number for measure.

The waiter was young and inexperienced. "Perhaps Monsieur would not mind paying cash . . ."

The glass turned slowly in MacFarlane's fingers — snapping at last under their pressure. He watched the thin trickle of blood with disbelief. A quick movement brought him to his feet, a head taller than the waiter. He knew the people at the next table were watching.

"Just open the bottle," he said self-consciously.

The waiter hesitated, mute apology in his eyes. Over the man's shoulder, MacFarlane saw the night manager and house detective standing at the hotel entrance. A chair grated behind him.

The Englishman was standing, towheaded in the moonlight. He spoke courteously to the waiter. "There seems to be some mistake — I was the one who ordered the champagne. This gentleman is my guest." He continued to stand as the waiter carried the bucket to his table. "Won't you join us, Mr. MacFarlane?"

The woman's eyelids lowered — she pulled the chair fractionally nearer. "Please sit down!" A thin brown hand held the armrest till MacFarlane was settled into the canvas. He watched her frankly, following the length of warm tanned arm to shoulder. She was wearing no rings.

The Englishman hooked his arms round the back of his chair. He had strong white teeth that he used when he smiled. "You don't know our names. This is Pia de Tellier — my name's Paul Anstey. Now you're wondering how I know who *you* are!"

MacFarlane took his time with the match. Sucked deep before exhaling the strong French tobacco. Something more primitive than reason ticked warning. He tried fitting the circumstances to his experience. What stood out as a pickup must surely be no more than late-night gregariousness. This girl — he corrected himself — this woman — was being friendly and that was all.

He answered when he was ready. "Should it matter that you know my name — what makes you think I'm curious?"

Anstey's laugh was big and easy. "Cannes is an odd place in season. I wanted you to be sure there was nothing sinister about it. You may have noticed us in the casino. We've been there every night for the past three weeks — most of the time watching the play at the big table. Watching you, in fact. When you left tonight, I asked the barman who you were. It was as simple as that."

MacFarlane settled deeper in his seat. Every casino had its batch of floaters. Gamblers who moved from table to table. Ever on the scent of the spectacular winner — the plunger in form. They took position behind your chair, breathing down your neck. Clutching pieces of paper covered with involved calculations. Communicating their own uncertainty till you either blew up or were forced to change seats.

He shrugged. "Don't tell me you're going to complain about my luck!"

Anstey plucked a thread from his knee. "I've always found it best to follow my own hunches. It's just as well. Every time I've opposed you, I've won."

The waiter was back bearing fresh glasses. He whispered in Anstey's ear as he poured. The blond man's face was puzzled. "Telephone?" He climbed to his feet, excusing himself.

The wine was good. Ice-cold bubbles exploded the need to think. MacFarlane drank it gratefully, attentive as the woman spoke.

Her voice was pleasantly pitched. "Are you an American, Mr. MacFarlane?"

She was probably in her late twenties, he judged. With no single feature you would call beautiful — save maybe the wide offset eyes. But a very female woman and incomparably sure of herself. For some reason, he found himself thinking of Sarah Whitaker's coquetry. A woman like this would find it unnecessary.

"I'm Canadian," he corrected.

She frowned slightly, the scar on her forehead white against her tan. "That is like the English and the Scotch — the difference, I mean. Very difficult for a foreigner." She held her glass sensibly, cupping its weight in her palms. Her interest robbed the question of impertinence. "And what do you do?"

The query had come earlier than he expected. For once it might be answered without having taken offense. "I'm a professional gambler."

His gravity seemed to amuse her. "But isn't one supposed

to be lucky to be a professional gambler, Mr. MacFarlane?"

Anstey was crossing the terrace. "It helps," answered the Canadian.

She hurried the words. "I hope your luck changes."

Something had taken the amiability from Anstey's face. MacFarlane watched him quizzically. Anstey sat down. "That was all nonsense about being wanted on the telephone. It was the detective and night manager." He looked over his glass. "They're worried about you!"

MacFarlane nodded. All that remained was to see how Anstey put an end to his gesture of hospitality. At least there had been that second glass of champagne.

"What did they tell you — that I'm a dangerous character?" He spoke pleasantly — the least he could do was help the guy off the hook.

Anstey looked uncertainly in the woman's direction. His fingers followed the crease in his trousers. "Not exactly. The whole thing was some sort of garbled warning. I suppose you know you've been locked out of your room?"

"Locked *and* padlocked," MacFarlane said. There was an idiotic second when he wanted to tell Anstey to relax. The man's concern was obvious. MacFarlane's hand showed the casino season ticket. "Even my passport's upstairs. I don't think this is too good a substitute."

Neither answered. The woman's eyes avoided him — he sensed her embarrassment. "There's no reason why you should have been dragged into all this. I apologize."

Anstey spoke with indignation. "That's nonsense! It's an impertinence in a hotel of this kind. I'm not sure that this business of holding your passport isn't illegal!"

MacFarlane stared where a creamy sea sucked at the sand.

11

"If it comes to that, I imagine it's illegal not to pay your bill." There seemed nothing more to be said.

Anstey was leaning back, eyes closed, hands gripped loosely behind his neck. "I told you I'd been watching your play. I hope you won't mind me saying this — but it takes more than nerve to gamble as you've been doing. For one thing, your opponents all have far too much money. The people you spoke to on the way out, for instance — the Whitakers. Do you know who he is?"

MacFarlane grinned. "He never stops reminding you of it." The truth was that Anstey was right. It took more than nerve and inspiration to stay in that company. Without a bankroll you were dead. All you could do was sit waiting for the one big coup that would bail you out of trouble. Never daring to call banco with money you needed for eating. Passing bank after bank till the *contrôle* padded over to hover at your elbow. Finally, needled by the official's suspicion, you went for some small bank without heart or hope. And lost. It had happened again tonight. The two months he'd spent on the Côte d'Azur had cost him ten thousand dollars.

MacFarlane found himself resenting the Englishman's shrewdness. To be exposed as a man temporarily unable to pay his hotel bill was one thing. For a complete stranger to have him pegged as a bluffer another.

Anstey still lolled, speaking with quiet confidence. "You couldn't have known this but it happens that I earn my living the same way as you do. I *have* to earn a living. I study my opponents, MacFarlane. Let me watch a man gamble for a week and I'll tell you his character. It doesn't take as long to know whether he can afford to lose. Every play you've made this past few weeks has shown that you were broke!"

Pia's hand was on the edge of MacFarlane's chair rest. If he touched it, he thought, it would be warm and responsive. She moved slim sunburned fingers. "Perhaps Mr. Mac-Farlane is waiting for another day."

There she was right. He thought of Thursday as a talisman to be tucked away securely. "There's *always* another day," he said slowly.

Anstey stretched, nodding vigorous approval. "The old maxim — your chance is never better than with the next throw of the dice. You know, MacFarlane, the only difference between us is that I've had a lot of luck this past couple of years. And I've used my head. There are two columns in my bookkeeping. One's for working capital — the other's for living expenses. I don't mix 'em up. Do you see my point — for me there always *is* another day!"

MacFarlane yawned. It was time to break up this two-men gambler's convention. To move on without giving affront. Where, exactly, he had no idea. The wine had given him no inspiration — merely lulled his sense of desperation. For that he was grateful. Maybe it would be best to walk for a while. There were still a few bars open in town — places where he could sit over a cup of coffee till morning. Later, there'd be still another trip to the *mont de pieté* — the state-run pawnshop near the station. He bent down and unstrapped his watch. He put it back on his wrist without comment.

Pia was on her feet, turning toward him. The smile flashed in her dark face. "Goodnight, Mr. MacFarlane. I hope we shall meet again." She gave him her hand. It felt as he knew it would — warm and friendly. Both men stood as she went into the hotel.

Anstey sat down carefully, pouring the last of the wine into MacFarlane's glass. "What are you going to do about a bed?"

MacFarlane shrugged. He was getting bored with the Englishman's persistent interest. He heard his words slur with indifference — recognizing the effect of the wine.

"Something will turn up — it always does." He found bogus assurance. "There'll be other pastures to graze."

The fair man shook his head. "That's just booze talking. I don't think you believe it yourself. It's gone three. You haven't a razor — a change of clothes — not even a clean shirt. Where do you think you'll go dressed like that? How much is your bill here?" His voice was casual.

MacFarlane emptied his glass deliberately, the bubbles sharp on his tongue. "You're beginning to bother me. I can't make up my mind whether you're a gentleman from the police — a tourist out for kicks — or even what you claim to be. Not that it matters too much. Whichever way you play it, you're entitled to value for your champagne."

The Englishman smiled. "I'm getting it!"

MacFarlane's look was knowing. "Sure — you're the man who never makes a mistake. That's why you want to know how come I'm sitting here broke. I don't mind telling you — it'll make you feel still better." He held the pawn tickets like a poker hand, flipping one after another on the table. "Gold cigarette case — lighter. A pair of Zeiss field glasses. All part of the gentleman gambler's equipment." He emptied his pockets of change. "Four hundred francs. That and an invitation to play baccarat at the Whitakers on Thursday.

Are you an amateur of irony, Mr. Anstey?" He caught his hiccough.

Anstey's wallet was open. "I asked you how much your bill was, here."

"One hundred thirty-four thousand francs. Do you think the service is worth twenty per cent?"

Anstey counted out three hundred-dollar bills. "That'll pay for your room." He added two more bills and pushed the money across the table. "This is insurance that you'll be able to eat. I suggest you go in and deal with the night manager."

MacFarlane was studying the money as if it were fake. Though the sheaf of bills was close to his hand he made no attempt to take it. His voice was pleasant.

"And what is your angle?"

Anstey touched the back of his hand to his mouth, stifling a yawn. "If there is one, why not let it ride till lunchtime. I'd like you to lunch with me, MacFarlane. How about one o'clock at the Carlton?"

MacFarlane's eyes narrowed. "That's odd — I'd have bet money on it being the Carlton. What makes you so sure I'll be there. I'm a highly dubious character, you know."

Anstey stood. "You need sleep. As for the money — you're a bloody fool if you don't take it!"

MacFarlane caught the edge of the table, stopping himself from swaying. He wadded the money into a hip pocket. "Not *that* much of a bloody fool! One o'clock at the Carlton."

Anstey nodded toward the lighted entrance. "It's none of my business but in your place I wouldn't bother acting the outraged guest. I told the night manager that you're a friend of mine. It could be useful." His hand fell in salute. He walked off, his back square and reliable.

MacFarlane sat down unsteadily. He no longer tried to control the surge of excitement he knew so well. The hunch that flouted all known factors. A hundred times he had experienced the same flooding confidence. From high on the grandstand, binoculars jammed against his eye, following a horse down the backstretch. At a roulette table, sitting with averted head, listening to the click of the ball on the slowing wheel. It was the instinctive certainty that fortune was with him. And when the Fate Sisters beckoned, you followed.

He took his time going into the hotel. Placing one foot carefully in front of the other, his expression dignified. The next few minutes promised satisfaction. The night manager was behind the desk, seemingly lost in a list of bookings. He looked up as MacFarlane neared.

The Canadian smiled. Buzzards — the lot of them. With a sense of the expedient that never failed. He pulled his bill out — laid it on the counter together with the money Anstey had given him.

"I'd like to pay this. You won't mind changing some dollars?"

The porter scrambled up, skipping aside as the manager almost trod on his toes. Peugeot's head cocked like a bird's.

"I am entirely at Monsieur's service!" He manipulated a small calculating machine with dexterity. Stamping and receipting the bill, he placed it gently in front of MacFarlane. "I hope that Monsieur will accept my deepest apologies for any inconvenience this matter may have caused. As I have already explained — the instructions were not mine alone.

Monsieur will agree — every hotel must have its rules!" His hands spread wide.

MacFarlane counted his change meticulously. He tucked a sheaf of ten-thousand bills in an inner pocket. "As a matter of interest — is it one of your rules that when a guest can't pay his bill on demand you inform his friends?"

Peugeot pushed the question away from him with both hands. For the first time he showed discomfiture.

"I was not aware that you and Monsieur Anstey were acquainted. I sought for the best and can only repeat my apologies. Perhaps in view of the circumstances, Monsieur would like to make other arrangements?"

MacFarlane's voice was derisive. "In midseason? I don't think so — the service is lousy but I still like the view."

He followed the porter across the lobby. Peugeot's reflection appeared in twenty mirrors — head slightly bent as if he listened for something. Upstairs, the porter pulled a small key from an envelope and unlocked the padlock. The broken sealing wax spattered his sleeve. He brushed it off and opened the door with a flourish. His voice cracked slightly. *"Bonne nuit,* Monsieur MacFarlane!" He lingered.

The weight of the door hung in MacFarlane's hand. He swung it tentatively. *"Bonne nuit,"* he said at last. "You know what's wrong with your feet — you don't get enough exercise!" He closed the door gently.

His white matching bags had been piled against the bathroom door. The clothesclosets were empty. He opened cases, rehanging suits, stacking shirts. One small locked bag was untouched. He spread its contents on the bed. Passport — two ebony boxes with dice — a few snapshots, their edges yellowed and scuffed. He repacked the bag, handling each article with care. When he had brushed his teeth, he filled the bath with hot water, leaving the silk suit swinging on a hanger in the steam.

Cutting the lights, he lay on the bed's unturned covers. Somewhere in this hotel, Pia and Anstey were sleeping. For all he knew together and even on this same floor. He kicked over, unable to get the woman out of his mind. He told himself he had reached the age of thirty-seven without that sort of involvement. By accepting the fact that what most women wanted he was unable to offer — security. The others he'd taken or left with a deliberate policy of disengagement. Those who belonged to other men you left alone. A principle that paid on a long haul.

Sun slit the curtains, disturbing his sleep. He showered, his body alive to the shock of cold water. Wrapping himself in the toweling robe, he went out to the balcony. To the left across the bay, the contours of the islands were hidden in heat haze. The Croisette below improbable in the glittering sunlight. The sea was too blue — the raked sand too clean and unblemished. Even the parked cars looked like entries for a *Concours d'Elégance*. Directly beneath the balcony an orange parasol shaded the place where he had sat with Anstey. It was eleven o'clock.

He rang for orange juice, coffee and toast. He ate with the sun hot on his back, a floppy white hat shielding his eyes from the glare. He welcomed the thought that it was Wednesday. There was enough left of the money Anstey had given him to ensure a decent entrance at the Whitakers tomorrow.

He sprawled in the heat thinking of it all. He might

even increase his stake before play started at the baccarat table. There was always some confident drunk ready with a poker-dice cup. Guys like that were a gift. You took them with a sense of fairness and the odds. Playing according to the book — that was all that was necessary. That and stay-ing sober. With any sort of luck, he'd sit down sure of being able to call one good banco. And one good bank was what he needed.

There was the enigma of Anstey. Suppose he took the man at his own valuation — the Englishman's behavior was still odd. A gambler might buy a loser a drink. Fair enough. If he wasn't in the game, maybe he'd go as far as staking a guy to another hand in a poker school. But the conven-tions were limited. Nobody gave a stranger five hundred dollars under the Old Pals Act.

He finished the last of the ice-cold juice. The first ciga-rette of the day smoked strong and pungent. A few hours and he'd have the answer to Anstey's generosity. He flicked the fat ash, thinking of his brother. Certainly he wouldn't have been able to raise five dollars in that quarter — let along five hundred. Right now, Philip would be high in his air-conditioned office overlooking the Champs-Elysées. Con-scientiously leafing his way through agency reports. Keep-ing his faith with fifty contracts. There were people back in Canada who molded their export policies on Philip's judg-ment. Maybe he had dug too often and too deep in that vein.

He pitched the butt away, coming to his feet as he watched the slim brown body under a beach hat cross the hotel forecourt. The cop's whistle shrilled, white accouter-ments flashing as he held the traffic for Pia's passage. She picked her way across the hot asphalt, long-legged and un-hurried. Once past the steps leading down to the hotel beach, she vanished from MacFarlane's sight. Standing just inside the room, he watched the stretch of sand where she had to emerge. A beach boy, oiled black, carried her mat-tress to the edge of the water.

MacFarlane moved quickly, grabbing a towel, donning shorts. For a second he stood in front of the full-length mirror, mocking his own expectancy. Then running along the corridor, he caught an elevator on its way down.

He walked through burning sand to where she was. Put-ting his mattress by hers, he propped himself on an elbow. She lay motionless, ankles together, arms flat by her sides. Small pads of cotton covered her eyes.

He spoke quietly, trying not to startle her. "Good morn-ing!" Only the movement of her flat brown stomach be-trayed her breathing.

He tried again. In spite of the wish to use her name, he balked. "Good morning!"

She pulled the pads from her eyes. Shading her face with her hands, she half turned. In the light of day her tanned face showed fined white lines from nose to mouth. Her eyes were not black as he remembered them but the color of dark laurel. She shook her head, combing the hair from her face with one hand.

"Good morning! I'm sorry — I did not recognize your voice."

He tucked both legs under him, squatting to face her. "Why should you? How did you sleep?"

She stretched her legs, curling long painted toes. "I al-ways sleep well." She pushed into the warm sand, dribbling it through her fingers. " 'Sleep comes from a contented mind,' " she quoted. She ran her hand across the sand, obliterating the pattern she had made. "Do you have this saying in English, Mr. MacFarlane?"

He watched her hesitantly. She used her words like feelers. He had the sense of being probed far beyond their surface value. "Very probably. I wouldn't know much about contented minds but I sleep." He rolled over to his stomach, opening the blue pack of cigarettes. His curiosity about her relationship to Anstey was beyond reason. But so was everything else in this setup. He used the Englishman's name easily enough. "How's Paul this morning?"

She shook her head, frowning into a hand mirror. "I haven't seen him. I think he always sleeps well too." She wadded the tissue and sat up straight.

He pushed the spent match back in its box, irritated by the need to know whether or not Anstey was her lover. Her answer could have meant anything. "You know I'm having lunch with him?" he asked suddenly.

Her face showed neither surprise nor interest. "Then I can assure you it will be a very good lunch." She locked hands round her ankles, narrowing her eyes against the reflection of sun on water. "Do you swim?"

"Not unless I can help it. Maybe six times a year. And preferably in tepid water." He gestured at the raft that was moored fifty yards out. A boy, copper-skinned and agile, jackknifed expertly into the blue swell. "There's the answer. I don't like doing anything I don't do well."

She looked up under dark swinging hair. "I can understand that. What *do* you do well, Mr. MacFarlane? Tell me about yourself. I find you — well, bizarre." Nibbling her

21

lip, she rejected the word. *"Intrigant!* You do not like people — is that right?"

He buried the butt in the sand. "If you mean people in general, hell, no! I've got to know somebody to either like or dislike."

She turned the corners of her mouth down. "I feel squashed."

He stared out to sea, ashamed of his pose. A mile out in the bay, a speedboat was fussing round the stern of a fat white yacht. He recognized the vessel as belonging to people he'd met at the Whitakers'. Sam Slade, who spread his Hollywood aura with charm and benevolence. His wife apparently dedicated to its destruction. They'd both be at Thursday's party.

She scraped her hair back, looking at him thoughtfully. "Cannes is full of beautiful women, Mr. MacFarlane. And you are alone. Why is that?" She twisted her hair in a knot, holding a tortoiseshell pin between her teeth. She skewered the glossy bun and looked up. "Yet you are attractive to women!" The statement was almost impersonal and devoid of coquetry.

He grunted. "That depends what you mean by 'attractive'. I don't have any time for romantic complications. Right now, I don't have the money either."

She moved impatiently. "That has nothing to do with it. A woman need not even approve to be interested. I don't think you are used to Frenchwomen. Often we speak . . ." She sought inspiration gracefully, fingers fluttering. "Is 'objectively' the right word?"

"I'm not used to *any* women," he said shortly. "They're not part of a gambler's equipment. Not normally, that is." The shot was deliberate.

"I suppose that means Paul. He needs nobody to apologize for him, Mr. MacFarlane. Least of all me. I imagine you don't believe in friendship either."

He was disturbed by her sudden seriousness. "I believe in self-interest — OK, if you want to give it another name."

She eyed him steadily. "I think I prefer it."

He had the sudden need to defend himself. "It's a question of semantics — words, Pia. You do something for somebody — 'what a friend!' people say. But deep down, it's nothing but self-interest." He wiped the patch of sweat from his neck. "Everything is," he finished heavily.

Her dark eyes were curious. "With those ideas you must lead a very lonely life. You already know my first name — will you tell me yours?"

He got to his feet, grinning down at her. "Neil! A day like this, being lonely has its compensations. Do you want to take that swim now?"

She climbed up locking one knee behind the other. "You change your mind quickly."

He nodded. "In mid-air — if I think I'm doing myself some good!"

She used a good fast crawl. Her hair, bursting its knot, trailed wet on her shoulders. Gasping, he spurted to catch her. Beyond the raft, they rolled over on their backs and floated, staring up at an eggshell blue sky.

"Paradise," he said slowly. "And for fifty miles there isn't a hundred yards of beach that's free." He sculled himself nearer her. "I suppose you'll be moving on somewhere else pretty soon."

Her chin was high above the shallow swell. Slender painted toes bobbed as she moved brown legs lazily.

"Did you know Anstey paid my hotel bill this morning?"

23

Her hand drifted nearer his. "Did he — I had no idea but it's like him."

He had the feeling she was lying.

The wash of a passing boat carried them together. He grasped the outstretched hand without haste. For a second her fingers tightened, then they drifted apart.

Back on the beach, they dried vigorously, sharing his towel. Mopping her back, he found himself protesting his naïveté. If this was to be an affair, it must be kept casual. He had sudden distaste for the memory of Sarah Whitaker. Everything there would be too easy. A couple of days ago there had seemed worse ways of spending the fall than as the Whitakers' house guest.

He wrapped the damp towel round his neck. "I've got to go and meet Anstey. Look, can you have a drink with me this evening?"

"*Can* I?"

"OK, will you?" he amended. "Unless you're doing something else."

She combed her wet hair, her shoulders a darker gold than the sand on them. She smiled suddenly. "You mean with Paul! We're like an old and successfully married couple. Content to make no demands on one another." She propped her chin in her palm, looking up. "I would *like* to have drinks with you."

He stood gauche and uncertain. "Shall we make it here in the hotel — about seven?"

She rolled over on her back, replacing the cotton pads on her eyelids. "At seven," she promised.

He chose his clothes carefully. The silk suit and shirt were cool and without weight. Knotting the narrow tie, he

24

stood back and considered himself in the long mirror. A bit thin in the face, maybe. Summer had taken its toll. Long siestas that left him heavy-headed and without appetite. It would be different with the coming of winter. He took pleasure in the thought. The English racetracks, green and brown in the pale sunshine. White-railed straights with vistas of tall fences lost in the mist. The crude bars stuffy with red-faced men in checksuits. The blanketed horses in the paddock whinnying their excitement. No, winter was a better time. And you made a living with better people.

He took money, keys and passport. On an impulse, he went to the balcony. Pia was where he had left her, lying with head cradled in her arms, her shoulders to the sun.

The Carlton terrace was crowded. He made his way through jammed tables to where Anstey waved from a corner. Taking the proffered chair, he sat down, his whole body taut with excitement.

"Here I am — surrendering to my bond."

Anstey was even squarer in gray gabardine. Outsize sunglasses hid his eyes, the jutting cheekbones. The straw hair was brushed to schoolboy smoothness. "How about a drink?" he suggested cheerfully. There was a glass of whisky in front of him.

MacFarlane shook his head. "I'll stick to coke." He looked covertly at Anstey's hands, compact and solid. Dark hair covered the stubby fingers to the first knuckle. Without thinking, he compared them with his own. Slim and with the forefingers set at an exaggerated angle.

"I was down on the beach," he said idly, "talking to Pia." He used the name deliberately.

Even at three feet it was impossible to get past the barrier of tinted glass. Anstey smiled politely.

25

"And how is she this morning?"

Without waiting for an answer, he took the bottle from the waiter and filled MacFarlane's glass. "As far as I'm concerned this stuff's a dead loss unless it's mixed with rum. You seem nervous — are you?" he asked suddenly.

MacFarlane shook his head. Anstey had chosen the wrong word. He stared at the top of Anstey's head with apparent indifference. Deep in the precise parting, a few hairs showed black at the roots.

"No, I'm not nervous," he answered. If Anstey chose to dye his hair it was his business. But the knowledge gave MacFarlane a curious satisfaction.

Anstey's mouth was judicious. "Getting back to Pia . . ." He thought for a moment. "I don't quite know how to say this. His broad gleaming smile was wry. "I think of her as a sister. It isn't the sort of relationship I expect people to believe in. But I do ask them to respect it."

A flying wedge headed by two waiters pushed through the crowd. Head and shoulders above his wife, Sam Slade was making his confident way to a table bearing a card RESERVED. He returned MacFarlane's salute courteously.

Anstey's face tilted. "Someone you know?"

"A Hollywood wheel — one of the big ones. I've met him a couple of times at the Whitakers'." For some reason Slade's gesture gave him pleasure.

"This business about Pia . . ." In no way was he going to get involved in any heavy-brother drama. "I've asked her to have drinks with me this evening. You're welcome if you'd care to come."

"Suppose we eat," Anstey answered. "We can talk about that later." He called a waiter and paid the check.

They sat at a corner table overlooking the Croisette. Mac-Farlane picked his way through a good plain lunch that the Englishman did justice to. Coffee and a cigar seemed to give Anstey decision. He dribbled smoke reflectively. "I suppose we'd better talk about the angle. Of course you were right — there had to be an angle."

MacFarlane pushed long legs under the table, relaxed. "Of course."

"You're probably a better gambler than I am," Anstey offered. "And you know the Whitakers. I think you could make a killing there tomorrow night. Here's my offer. Whatever stake you need for that party, I'm prepared to find. The profits we split even-stephen."

The room had emptied. Save for a group of waiters at their service cart MacFarlane and Anstey were alone. Mac-Farlane's voice was noncommittal. "It's an interesting proposition. It gives me the chance to get out of your debt — that's important to me. There's another thing — I *know* I can make a killing." He kept his gaze steady over the top of Anstey's head. "There's only one snag I see."

The Englishman took his cigar from his mouth, viewing the wet end with distaste. "And what is it?"

"The bankroll," said MacFarlane. "If it's an average Whitaker party there'll be anything up to twenty people there." He nodded out at the bay. "The Slades — Lady Stowe — the Haggertys. Out of that twenty, you can figure that eighteen will come prepared to lose — say, three thousand dollars a head on the night's play. These people use real money, no checks, no markers."

Blue smoke hid Anstey's mouth. "Eighteen from twenty. What about the other two?"

MacFarlane tapped himself on the chest. "I'm one. And there's always some happy soul with his nose in a whisky bottle."

Anstey took a long time polishing his sunglasses. "I don't follow your argument. As long as you're bankrolled, where's the snag?"

MacFarlane's hand lifted. "You won't be there to see your money at work," he said simply. "Isn't that going to worry you?"

Anstey donned the glasses. "It's a point. I suppose there's no chance of me crashing the game?"

MacFarlane laughed. "Look, you've got to forget any private party you ever played at. This is different. The Whitakers are protected twenty-four hours a day. Not against gamblers, but cranks and burglars." He sat up, memory giving force to his explanation. "People like the Whitakers are your modern feudalists. They're generous to their servants but they expect blind obedience. And they get it. Without an invitation you wouldn't get your nose past the lodge gates." He grinned. "Not unless you happened to be a second-story man — and at that . . ." He recalled the long driveway in the early hours of the morning. The quiet gray car that took him home. The men and dogs as they passed, motionless in the shadow of the pines. "You can forget that," he said briefly.

Anstey was unperturbed. "Well, suppose we *were* invited! You know these people well enough to suggest it. A couple of your friends who'd like to play baccarat. It would make it even more of a certainty. Playing together, we could take twenty thousand dollars out of a game like that." He hitched his chair closer. "With me in the game, playing for you, we don't even *need* luck."

"I've seen it happen," remembered MacFarlane. "You say you can't lose, but you do. I don't know what sort of bankroll you've got in mind. It isn't just a question of matching their money. Are you prepared to lose it?" His look was direct.

Anstey moved impatiently. "Let me ask you a question, MacFarlane. What sort of scruples have you got?"

"Suppose you give me an example," MacFarlane said warily.

Anstey leaned across the table confidentially. "You say yourself all these people come prepared to lose three thousand dollars. Money means nothing to them. There's one way it's possible to win and impossible to lose. We call the first big bank — if it comes our way we play up the profits. If we lose . . ." He lifted a shoulder. "We excuse ourselves and say goodnight."

MacFarlane's shock was genuine. "Without paying?"

"Without paying," said Anstey coolly.

It was true. In any casino it was true. No money changed hands at a baccarat table till a bank was lost or won. If you lost, nothing prevented you leaving the place without paying. The worst that could happen would be a red tab on your dossier. But once that happened you'd never get past the entrance of any European casino again.

He tried for honesty. "It isn't a question of scruple, Anstey — just expediency. I can't afford to be blacklisted where I make my living."

Anstey was grinning. He took another cigar from a crocodile case. "You've given me the answer I wanted. Sorry if I had you going for a moment. Don't give it another thought. I want you in that game with nothing on your mind but the intention of winning." He lit the slender

29

brown tube. "The truth is that a thousand pounds won't either make or break me. Let's leave it at that." He whipped off his glasses. The blue eyes were out of focus. "Is it a deal or not?" he asked.

"A thousand pounds," MacFarlane repeated slowly. He shook his head. "I thought you meant a big bank."

Anstey shrugged. "There'll be a reserve. I just want to make it plain what I'm prepared to lose. Well?"

MacFarlane climbed from his chair, his decision taken.

"OK. It's a deal. It means I'll have to phone Sarah Whitaker right away. You'd better come with me."

It took ten minutes and all MacFarlane's patience to reach the Whitakers. It was hot in the booth. Anstey's square bulk filled the doorway.

Sarah Whitaker's voice was puzzled. "*Where* do you say you're speaking from, Neil? I can hardly hear you. It sounds exactly as though you're frying bacon."

He bent over the mouthpiece, as solicitous as if she were there with him. "I'm sorry to bother you, Sarah. But I ran into a couple of friends last night at the casino. It seems they've been here a week or so. I didn't even know they were here." He held the receiver away from his ear, making a face at Anstey. "It's a woman *and* a man," he said patiently. "*Yes*, they're amusing. As a matter of fact I was wondering about them coming tomorrow night. Both of them like to play."

A door shut at the other end of the line. "Are you alone?" she asked.

"Yes. Shall I bring them or not, Sarah? If it's a drag, forget it."

"Bring them by all means if you want to," she answered indifferently. "Are you alone?" she repeated.

"Unless you count the switchboard girl — I don't think she's listening but how can you tell!"

Her voice wheedled. "Neil — why don't you bring a bag with you. Stay over till Monday? The Slades are sailing their boat down to Amalfi. George is thinking of going with them."

The offer was tempting. There were bridle paths deep in pine needles — to walk or to ride. At the end of the day, mountain water in a pool warmed by the relentless sun. And the problem of Sarah Whitaker. He was finding her approach neither subtle nor obscure.

Anstey was watching intently, holding both sides of the door frame. MacFarlane turned his head away. "I'm not going to be able to do that, Sarah. Look, be reasonable, these friends are only here for a few more days. How about next weekend?"

By then he should be a thousand miles away with enough money to see him through the winter.

Her laugh was indulgent. "All right — Neil!" He screwed his mouth against the inevitable coyness. "It'll seem a long time."

He left the booth and paid for the call. His shirtfront felt clammy. He noticed with amazement the faint shake in his hand. They stood on the steps leading down to the Croisette.

"You heard it — you're both invited." MacFarlane watched the other man's expression — hiding his own wariness.

"Fine," said Anstey absentmindedly. "How do we go on for transport?"

"They'll send a car to the hotel — sevenish and you dress."

"Perfect, I can put the Jag in for servicing." The Englishman grinned. "How long are we supposed to have known one another?" He moved down a step, letting a woman pass. From above, the few dark roots were obvious.

"Better say a couple of years. It's quite possible, she'll pump you about me — tell her what you like."

Anstey's smile was conspiratorial. "From what I heard she'd prefer to get her information at first hand." He winked. "You could do worse."

MacFarlane found the suggestion too near the truth to be acceptable. He was beginning both to dislike and mistrust Anstey. He followed him down to the sun-scorched street resolved on one thing. The money they played with would stay under his control. He had no intention of creating a scandal that might ruin him professionally.

Anstey's bulk blocked the sidewalk. "Which way do you go?"

MacFarlane jerked his head. "Back to the hotel. I need as much sleep as I can get between now and tomorrow night."

They walked together, past crowded bars where half-naked people sat, stupid with food and sun. The slim gold case and matching lighter in Carter's window were replicas of his own. He was thinking of Friday morning with confidence. Somehow the picture of Pia persisted through the vision of paid bills and property redeemed.

Once in his room, MacFarlane stripped and drew the shades. He was almost dozing when a familiar roar took him to the balcony window. The chasseur was maneuvering the white Jaguar into the forecourt. A moment later, Anstey appeared. A short-sleeved shirt topped his jeans. He threw a couple of bags in the back of the car and drove off.

32

MacFarlane slept heavily, waking to the phone's insistence.

He dressed in a hurry, changing his linen and suit. By the time he reached the terrace, Pia was already waiting. She was cool and elegant in lemon-colored shantung. Her long hair had been caught in a knot on her neck. Her slender neck bore her head with grace.

He bent over her hand. "It's a long time since I saw anything looking so good as you do tonight," he said honestly.

Sun gave her skin a patina. She moved a bare foot, dangling her sandal by the thong. "I think I see what Paul means about you. You show what you feel. That can hardly be good for a gambler!"

"OK — how about this — " He wore a dead-pan expression, his eyes china-blank.

She smiled, savoring the crushed mint that floated in the frosted glass. "That's better. It would be disastrous to know everything people are thinking. How was your lunch?"

He gave the waiter an order. "As you said it would be — good. Incidentally, I just saw Paul throwing bags in his car. Is someone leaving?"

She sat up straight, her eyes for a second hesitant. She was suddenly relaxed. "That would be the cleaning. Paul always takes it to the same place in Nice."

"Is that it!" He watched the pulse in her throat. "Don't you want to know what Paul had to say at lunch?"

She affected to think. "I might be able to guess."

It was a suggestion that she and Anstey had no secrets. And it irritated him. "All right — you know already. But this might be news. You're both invited to the Whitakers tomorrow night."

33

She was unmoved. "An honor. The fabulous Mrs. Whitaker." She smiled. "I watched her last night in the casino. You've made a conquest."

He moved uncomfortably. Her raillery followed too close on Anstey's. He imagined their joint amusement and found it unpleasant. "Sarah Whitaker's interested in herself," he said shortly.

"You make it sound a criticism — didn't you tell me everybody was?" The mockery was gentle yet definite. "Tell me about her, Neil. Is she pleasant?"

He took no pleasure in the prospect. "There's nothing to tell. She's forty-five and has too much money."

She tapped her teeth with a nail, considering him.

"That's an answer for a man. Women are always curious about other women. Especially those who have too much money. According to the French newspapers, she bought half a Paris collection for herself. Do you think that would be true?"

He tried keeping his voice free of irritation. "It could be. I don't know what clothes she has — I've never been in her bedroom."

She laughed out loud. "My God — how seriously we're taking everything! You're answering me as if I were a jealous wife. I'm not really jealous of *anything* she has — not even her jewelry." She looked at her own ringless fingers.

Her wryness gave him the desire to console her. "I guess Sarah Whitaker's jewelry must be insured for more than a hundred thousand dollars. It doesn't seem to do much for her. A husband whose nose is never out of a gin bottle." He shrugged.

Her dark green eyes were thoughtful. "All the ingredients for happiness save one."

" 'Happiness' is a woman's word," he said roughly. "What the hell — their lives would be a lot tougher if he had to carry his lunch to work with him every day."

She was paying no attention. "Never to have to worry about stupid things like meals being cooked — houses cleaned. The dreary things women are supposed to enjoy. For the rich, all is done like magic."

He remembered the endless Whitaker servants. Discreetly unobtrusive yet anticipating every wish. "That's about what it is — twenty magicians with brooms and dusters. Tell me something, Pia. Where are you going after this?" His hand took in the crowded terrace — its tanned and pretentious patrons.

She met his look fairly. "I don't know, Neil. Wherever Paul decides. And you?"

"England. Winter in England! People think I'm crazy yet there's no other place I'd rather be." He leaned across the table, face bright with memory. "Each year I rent a little apartment in London. Not much more than a box with a bath, off Sloane Square. And every day there's racing I'm out at the track." He grinned. "I know all the guys on the racetrack special. The spivs, the bookmakers, owners and jockeys. England's always been lucky for me, Pia." He sought her face hoping to read some of his own enthusiasm.

Her forehead creased. "I've never been to England. Paul will not go back. There must be many like him. War heroes do a lot better to die," she finished quietly.

This trailing after Anstey all her life, preaching the gospel of his goodness, was an unnatural relationship. And she

35

was completely normal. It was as simple as that. Every move she made proclaimed her absolute femininity. He tried to evoke it.

"Were you ever married, Pia?" he asked suddenly.

"Yes."

"How about Paul?"

"He's been married too." She turned her head away, making it obvious she had no intention of saying more.

He watched her moodily. She seemed poised ready to run at the wrong word. He went carefully, because it mattered to him.

"You know Paul's staking me tomorrow night. I've got a feeling that I'm going to hit lucky. You can leave that sort of game with the whole course of your life changed."

She smoothed the silk over her thighs with nervous fingers.

"You believe in yourself. It is a great quality."

He sipped his drink slowly. It had to be the last till the party was over. When he gambled, he gave drink a miss. A precaution to be watched — anyone noticing it was likely to wonder. So you took Scotch after Scotch, forgetting them on the way from table to table.

"I won't lose," he said steadily. "*You've* got no problem. All you have to do is look the way you do now. Bet when you feel like it. The men'll be too interested in your legs to bother what your stake is. And the women too jealous to notice it."

She leaned back, round throat swelling as she laughed.

"I shall finish by believing those pretty speeches. And that could be dangerous." She looked at him innocently.

"I'll take a chance on it." He wanted to keep her like this — relaxed and responsive. "Why don't you have dinner with me? Do what you want to do for once!" he urged.

"How do you know it *is* what I want?" she asked reasonably.

His quick movement sent the glasses on the table clattering.

"It is — you know it is! Pia . . ." People were turning their heads. He lowered his voice. "Please, Pia!"

She peered into her hand mirror, outlining the red curve of her mouth. The clasp of her bag snapped shut. "I can't, Neil. I have to eat with Paul. It was already arranged."

His lips twisted. "You *can't!* What you really mean is that you're not allowed to eat a meal with a stranger, isn't it!"

She finished her drink with composure. "Your manners are quite bad at times, my friend. And your suggestion stupid. Ask Paul yourself." She pointed to where Anstey was crossing the terrace almost as if on cue.

MacFarlane looked up guardedly. Fresh sun had burned the Englishman's face red under the brown. "Sit down and have a drink," MacFarlane invited. "I've just been trying to persuade Pia to have dinner with me. I was unsuccessful." He shaded the sun from his eyes, craning up at Anstey. "Do you know there's straw all over your back?"

Anstey's head turned with astonishing rapidity. He used the backs of his hands to brush the wisps of straw from his dark blue shirt. Politeness required an obvious effort. "Thanks. There was probably straw in the garage." His blunt fingers touched Pia's shoulder possessively. "Ask her some other time. I had priority." His square body was completely at ease again. The broad smile made a confidant of MacFarlane. "Don't forget I've got to raise six thousand dollars in cash by tomorrow night. This one takes care of my banking. It needs talking about. You won't mind if we shove off?"

MacFarlane hauled himself to bend over Pia's hand, brushing her skin with his mouth deliberately. He straightened, aware of Anstey's tight smile. "Goodnight, Pia! This time I'll give you plenty warning. How about the day after tomorrow?"

She was standing a little in front of Anstey. "I shall be very happy, Neil."

The Englishman collected her arm. "Let's hope you've got something to celebrate," he said dryly. Brushing the remaining straw from his jeans, he turned away.

Long after they were gone, MacFarlane sat in front of an empty glass. The sun dipped behind the Esterels, the last of its light touching the rocks blood-red. He paid his bill and walked up to the Rue d'Antibes. A small restaurant provided a meal that he ate without pleasure. He was too excited to either sleep or eat. It was one o'clock before he went to his room.

Thursday dragged itself out. In the afternoon Anstey telephoned MacFarlane's room with the news that six thousand dollars in cash had been promoted. MacFarlane put the phone down with relief. In spite of Anstey's front, the doubt that he was bluffing had always been there. For the rest of the day he saw nothing of either of them.

The sun was low when he left his room to go downstairs. Pia and Anstey were waiting on the terrace. The Englishman was sober in black jacket and tie. He sat with a briefcase across his knees. MacFarlane joined them, shaking his head as Anstey pointed at the whisky in front of him.

"I'd take it easy on that stuff," MacFarlane advised. "Once you get up there you'll never have a glass out of your hand."

"I know what I'm doing." Anstey picked fastidiously at his shirtfront. The flush on his face had faded. "It's past seven — how long are we going to wait for this car?"

MacFarlane considered them both speculatively. Pia was wearing a short dress the color of old gold. Her hair had been piled almost casually on top of her head. A deep brocade bag hung on the side of her chair. She seemed to look everywhere save at the Englishman. Something's happened between them since yesterday, thought MacFarlane. The strain showed in Anstey's brusqueness — her silence. He found himself wondering if they had quarreled. With keener interest, if they had quarreled over him.

A gray Rolls was turning into the forecourt. MacFarlane jerked his head. "There's the car. Come on — let's go."

By the time they reached the Rolls, the chasseur had the door open. Beyond the glass front of the hotel, the night manager was trying to dissemble his curiosity. MacFarlane climbed in after Pia, Anstey taking the seat on the far side.

The chauffeur's head turned. "I'm afraid I'm a couple of minutes late, sir. Got 'eld up at the lights over the railway bridge."

His cockney accent was strange and reminiscent. He wore gray livery matching the color of the car. "Is it all right if I put me foot down a bit going home, sir? I got another trip to make right away. To Hyères." He pronounced it High Ears with no concession to a foreign language.

MacFarlane grinned at him. "Just as long as you get us there in one piece."

39

They sat silent as the Rolls ghosted its way east then turned, crossing the Rue d'Antibes. Pia was sitting very straight, her eyes closed. Her bag lay on the occasional seat in front of her. Surreptitiously MacFarlane shifted his weight bringing his thigh against hers. She was completely unresponsive, intent apparently on whatever troubled her. Anstey smoked incessantly, filling the ash tray with smoldering butts.

MacFarlane considered him without pleasure. Sweat covered the Englishman's upper lip. He fidgeted too much, thought MacFarlane. He spoke to Anstey quietly, glancing at the soundproof glass division.

"Suppose we get this money business straightened out."

They were climbing the wide curving road to Grasse. The powerful motor propelled the heavy car with soundless speed. Anstey broke open his briefcase. A thin sheaf of thousand-dollar bills — a thicker wad of hundreds. He reached across Pia, throwing the roll to MacFarlane's lap. "Count it. There should be four thousand there. That'll do to start with."

The car swung out, overtaking a fat bus belching diesel fuel. With a sudden lurch, Pia's bag fell to the carpet. MacFarlane's reaction was a fraction faster than Anstey's. The two men's heads bumped at the level of the woman's knees. It was MacFarlane who retrieved the bag. He held it by the strap for a second then put it back on the seat in front of him.

"What have you got in there — a brick?" He grinned reassurance at her. "If it's a bottle, let's hope it's not broken." He felt her body relax.

Anstey's square fist knuckled his temple. "You've got a hard head," he said ruefully.

"They grow 'em that way in northern Ontario." Not for a thousand dollars would MacFarlane have touched the throbbing lump above his ear. "The ingredients are oatmeal, molasses and the fear of God. I was raised in a Caledonian Rite parsonage," he volunteered.

Already they were in the outskirts of Grasse, on the last wide bend before the crossroads. Above them blazed the banked lights of the terraced town. Beyond that, dark green mountains scarred with rock faded into the gathering night. Whining a little as the motor braked, the Rolls dropped down to the bridge marking the boundary between Alpes-Maritimes and Var.

Anstey had stopped chain-smoking. The solid bulk of his body seemed relaxed. "What time do you think the game'll get under way?"

MacFarlane considered. "There's usually a cold buffet first. Most of them eat out somewhere before they come." He shrugged, fingering the patch of hair over his ear, the bruise beneath it. "It could be eleven before we start."

The road hugged the wooded contours. Dense forests dropped toward the coastline in ever decreasing folds. Here and there a patch of poor earth showed by the roadside, desolate and weed-ridden. An abandoned *cabanon* was testimony to a relinquished struggle. Suddenly they were at the head of a long straight road dropping to the plain. He gestured through the window at the stone-built wall. "Everything the other side of that belongs to the Whitakers."

The car turned off the highway where a lodge and gate protected a graveled driveway. With the sound of the horn, a man in forester's uniform came to the open lodge door. Recognizing the car, he swung a lever. The white gate rolled on its hinges. As they passed the lodge, Anstey pointed at the shotgun propped against the wall.

"What are they expecting — a revolution?"

"There's a plaque somewhere in Draguignan that says *'George Whitaker. Benefactor of our country.'* He gave fifty million francs relief after the forest fires. Now he does pretty well as he likes hereabouts. A couple of months ago, one of the guards he's got working for him shot an Algerian." He nodded at the woods, purple in the changing light. "Over there! Nobody even bothered calling Whitaker into Draguignan."

Two miles on, the drive expanded into three acres of grassland. Fronted by a formal English garden, a stone-built house straggled over fifty yards. As the car drew in beside the other vehicles, dogs set up a racket from the back of the house. Coach lanterns lighted welcome at the head of the shallow steps. The heavy embossed door was thrown open at the moment they reached the top step. The waiting manservant spoke serviceable English. "Good evening, sir. May I have your names?"

He checked them against a list on the side table.

"Please — will you come this way?"

The long hall extended the width of the house, cool and quiet. Pewter glowed on the white walls. They followed the manservant to an alcove. There were two doors. On one was fastened an ivory fan, on the other a giant cigar holder. A smiling maid took Pia's black velvet cloak.

MacFarlane closed the door behind him. Anstey was scrubbing short nails with care, his back to MacFarlane. He used the monogrammed brushes, smoothing the blond wings over his ears.

"Are these maids and people meant to sit up half the night waiting for us?"

MacFarlane dusted a speck from his white jacket. God, he thought, how sick you could get at the sight of your own face. Thin, strained — and in spite of the tan, puffy about the eyes. It would take a month's racing to straighten him out. He needed the wind, rain and sun of an English fall.

He pitched the soiled towel in a basket. "Don't lose any sleep about the help here. Everyone goes to bed as soon as we've eaten," he answered. "The Whitakers get 'em out of the way." He retied his bow, equalizing the ends. "Sarah takes her Lady Bountiful role pretty seriously. She worries about scandal. She has to. Last time I was up here, some Brazilian got loaded and kept threatening to shoot himself with George's gun."

"What did they do with *him?*" asked Anstey dryly. "Feed him to the dogs?"

MacFarlane had the door open. "Put him to bed. Only not before he blew half his big toe off."

Pia was waiting in the hall.

"In here — " He pointed at the cream-painted door at the end of the hall. He turned the handle on a room fifty feet long — almost half as wide. Lettuce-green silk curtains were still undrawn in two wide windows overlooking the front of the house. In the deep fireplace between them, an olive trunk smoldered. He stood aside to let Anstey pass, then took Pia's arm. Except for the Slades and Whitakers he knew none of the dozen people already there. Beyond the buffet table, George Whitaker was shaking drinks in professional manner.

Sarah Whitaker hurried toward them, both hands outstretched.

"Neil!" Before he could avoid it, her cheek was pressed against his. "And these are your friends." She turned from Pia to Anstey, bright eyes losing no detail. "How nice of you to come!"

"Do you know Paul Anstey . . ." MacFarlane started automatically.

Mrs. Whitaker's smile for Anstey was dazzling. "But we've met surely! Now where?" She continued her inspection of Pia, holding her smile. "Mrs. Anstey's far too striking to be forgotten."

MacFarlane moved nervously. "This is Pia de Tellier — Mrs. Whitaker."

Anstey's manner was perfect. He was neither intimidated nor gushing. "It's kind of you to ask us. We've been in Cannes a few days without knowing that Neil was there. As a matter of fact we ran into him in the casino last night." His wide grin was friendly. "It's possible you might have noticed us there."

Mrs. Whitaker's hand moved gracefully, striking fire from the emerald-cut brilliant on her finger. "De Tellier! With that coloring you couldn't possibly be English!" The statement was just short of a criticism.

Pia hesitated. "I'm half French — half Italian." She made an effort, "No English, I'm afraid."

MacFarlane moved restlessly. Sarah must have had her maid working for hours. The rose-pink chiffon dress with its harem skirt left the famed Whitaker legs open to admiration. She kept lifting her head high so that her diamond-circled neck showed an unblemished line. The Queen

44

Mother, he thought. And nobody would be allowed to forget it.

He spoke doggedly, refusing to meet Pia's look.

"You look lovely, Sarah!"

Mrs. Whitaker shook her head, hooking an arm under his.

"Dear Neil!" She made as if to share her pleasure with the younger woman. "You know this man says the nicest things!"

The warmth of her arm was an embarrassment. He watched Pia's face apprehensively. He had to get these two women away from one another.

Pia's face was guileless. "On this occasion at least, he's absolutely right."

Mrs. Whitaker's hand freed MacFarlane. "You know where everything is, Neil. Get these charming people a drink." She stared at Anstey, lowering her lids. "We don't do much introducing at our little parties, Mr. Anstey, but let me start you off." She captured the Englishman's sleeve and led in the direction of Sam Slade's discreet boom.

MacFarlane watched her go, hiding his distaste. "Well, there it is," he said quietly. "That's what you wanted to see."

Pia shrugged, her face expressionless. "Nevertheless she is very rich."

Piano music filtered from speakers behind the tapestry on the wall. Whitaker was at his bar mixing enormous martinis. He looked past the shaker, closing one pink eye at Mac-Farlane.

"Ahah! A lovely lady I don't know."

"Pia de Tellier — George Whitaker." MacFarlane watched

45

his host's unsteadiness happily. Three more of those martinis on an empty stomach and Whitaker would be airborne.

"I'll take a Scotch, George." He smiled. "I don't trust your mixtures."

"For me, too, please." Pia was being very French for Whitaker. "You are so kind, having us here."

Whitaker swelled like a turkey. "Nonsense!" The heavy decanter trembled in his hand. "Is Miss de Tellier your lucky charm, Neil? I have a feeling you'll need one tonight." He lowered the cut-glass tumbler with drunken caution.

"Blowhard!" MacFarlane answered pleasantly. "We'll circulate for a bit, George!" Whitaker's fingers were disposed to linger on Pia's hand.

"Don't rush off." Whitaker came from behind his bar. He angled his head, peering down the front of Pia's dress.

"Miss de Tellier might bring me a little luck too."

His wife's voice straightened his back. "Swat George away if he bothers you," she called. "And don't trust his martinis." She stood under her own portrait, talking to Anstey and Slade.

MacFarlane blocked Whitaker with a shoulder, putting a hand on Pia's bare back. "Let's get something to eat."

Having her here was a mistake, he thought suddenly. Whitaker's alcoholic gallantry was harmless enough. He'd use any attractive woman in an attempt to shake his wife's indifference. It was Sarah Whitaker's reaction that was unpredictable. MacFarlane took Pia's arm, steering her away from trouble.

Behind the buffet table a pair of white-capped chefs waited for custom. MacFarlane looked at the mounds of food, his stomach queasy. Whole roasts of sucking pig, sides of ham, salmon and fowl, creamy fish in aspic. He swallowed, pointing at random. He pushed the untouched glass of whisky out of sight.

Champagne cooled in buckets behind the table. One of the men thumbed the cork from a bottle and filled two glasses. They carried their food to the far end of the room. The baize-topped table was ready for play. An unbroken carton of playing cards — the wooden shoe to hold them. A green-shaded lamp hung on an adjustable cord. Pia touched a button on the wall, flooding the table with light. Snapping off the button, she pushed the food about on her plate halfheartedly.

He leaned his back against the wall, visualizing her wrapped against the chill of an English winter. Walking beside him as they followed a winner to the unsaddling enclosure.

"Will you come to England with me, Pia?" he asked impulsively. Her laurel eyes were lowered. She was more nervous then he had ever seen her. "On your terms," he emphasized.

She looked down at the fork that hung limp in her fingers. He saw no more than the curve of her cheek — the dark smoothness of her hair. "That's nonsense — you don't even know me."

"I don't have to," he said obstinately. Surely she realized reason played no part in any of this.

She carried her plate to a side table. She looked at him slant-eyed, then emptied her glass. "I don't know you either," she said quietly.

The room had filled. Through the crowd at the buffet, Anstey's broad back was moving doggedly in the direction of

47

Mrs. Slade. MacFarlane watched as the Englishman halted. The woman's face was bright with interest as Anstey spoke to her.

"Are you going to go on chasing him all your life?"

MacFarlane was unable to keep the bitterness from his voice.

"I'm chasing nobody." She stood by the wall at his side. She shifted her bag from one arm to another. "We're not children, Neil. I find this sort of conversation useless."

He rubbed the side of his head nervously. "OK. I got what I asked for. I ought to have learned by now, God knows! What was the big build-up for?"

Her eyes widened. "Build-up! Now I really don't know what you're talking about. You've no idea how ridiculous you look when you scowl like that." She shook her head.

He was heavily sarcastic. "Is that right! I don't think it's too difficult to understand. Yesterday on the beach — in the water." He made a sound of disgust, slammed his glass down, anger destroying all sense of proportion. "I'm getting out of here now. I'll make some excuse to Sarah. You and Anstey can have it all on your own. Isn't that what it's all been in aid of!"

She held his wrist in her slim brown fingers. "You're being foolish, Neil. Acting like a jealous boy." They stood unnoticed as her lips brushed his cheek. "Like a small rebellious boy," she said softly.

He was leaning against the wall watching her, ashamed of his outburst and irritated by the ease with which she had dealt with it. She was able to make him appear gauche at will.

"I'll tell you something about rebels," he said with emphasis. "I don't expect you to know what this means, but I grew up in a God-fearing manse. They breed rebels there." He lowered his voice. "At fourteen, I believed that on Sunday anything but the Bible was sinful reading. Let me tell you something else I believed — all gamblers went straight to hell!"

She started to say something but he stopped her. "*Listen* — then perhaps you won't find this 'jealous boy' routine necessary! I worked twelve hours a day to put myself through college. I don't know why — I learned more in a lumber camp. And I never went home again. Keep that in your head when you're thinking about working on me. Now go ahead and say whatever it was you were going to say!"

She kneaded the skin where he had held her arm. "It doesn't matter. You say you never went home — why?"

He was careful to keep his voice free of emotion.

"Because there *was* no home — not for me, anyway. I gambled, I smoked and I drank. People back in Elgin still remember my father's sermon on the subject. A cliffhanger that lasted all winter." He dismissed the past without regret. "And I've been untroubled by conscience ever since! What I want you to understand is this — I meant exactly what I said about you coming to England with me on your terms. I'll ask you again tomorrow night."

She was playing with the light button again — flicking on the bulb that hung over the baccarat table — switching it off. Her voice was very quiet. She shook her head. "I don't think you will. And perhaps it is better."

It was a quarter to eleven. Servants busied themselves drawing curtains. Outside the gossiping chauffeurs stood by their parked cars, their cigarettes glowing in the darkness. Both chefs stood stiff and straight, grinning their pleasure at Sarah Whitaker's appreciation. Her face was flushed and she clung to Anstey's arm as if determined not to lose him.

MacFarlane watched with grudging admiration. He had no liking for Anstey — not even gratitude. The Englishman was too smooth — too full of surprises. And a benefactor. Nevertheless MacFarlane recognized a man with an eye to the main chance. Ah well, at least it kept Sarah Whitaker occupied.

When the doors had closed on the last servant, Mrs. Whitaker clapped her hands together. Her high clear voice stilled the babble. "People! People! We're going to start." She swiveled on her heel, picking out one person after another. "There are only seats for twelve. Some of you will have to stand and play." "Neil!" MacFarlane walked across to her. "I want you on one side of me." She turned to Anstey. "And you on the other."

The Englishman shook his head. "I think I'll stand for a bit if you don't mind. I'd like to get the rhythm of the play here first." He held Mrs. Whitaker's chair for her. MacFarlane sat on her right. All lamps save the one hanging over the table were out. MacFarlane blinked with the sudden change of lighting. His eyes still held the picture of Pia standing close to the wall.

Whitaker started to break the seals on the decks of cards. His wife had a small gold box on the table in front of her. MacFarlane could see the serried hundred-dollar bills inside. He dug in his pocket for money, his heart beating a little faster.

A woman shrieked as the room was plunged in darkness.

"It's a fuse — nobody panic!" It was Whitaker's voice.

The light over the table came on again. Anstey was standing behind Sarah Whitaker. A hand over her mouth held her head jerked back. The other held a short-barreled gun against her neck.

His voice was clear and precise. "All of you understand English. Nobody moves till I say so — and keep it quiet." He took his hand from Sarah Whitaker's mouth. Her head sagged.

MacFarlane kept his eyes on the table, clenching his fists till the muscles in his forearms ached. Across the green baize Pia was standing with her bag in one hand — in the other, the counterpart of Anstey's weapon.

The same woman screamed again, the sound dying faint in her throat. Anstey took a couple of steps to his right, chopping at the woman's head with his free hand. "Shut up, you fat bitch!" he said savagely. He balanced the automatic comfortably, holding it close to the back of Sarah Whitaker's neck. He bared strong white teeth. "If you'll all do as you're told, nobody gets hurt. If not — I'm quite ready to blow a few heads off."

MacFarlane felt the tremor in Mrs. Whitaker's body. Farther round the table a man collapsed with his head between his arms. Anstey ignored him. "All of you empty your bags and pockets of cash and jewelry. Put everything on the table in front of you. Don't bother holding out — I'll go through your pockets later." His face was amiable.

He walked over to the unconscious man, rolling the head to one side, thumbing back an eyelid. It was Sam Slade. Casually, Anstey tore the man's tie free and loosened his collar.

George Whitaker was the first to start emptying his pockets. His voice had a drunken bravado. "You won't get away with this, Anstey."

Anstey tapped the top of Whitaker's head with the gun barrel.

"Shut up, George, you talk too much." Whitaker's face paled. He flinched as Anstey bent over him, running his hands through his pockets.

As though by joint accord, men and women were piling money and jewelry on the table. Those who stood behind jostled those in front in their haste. Anstey made the round, collecting the cash and stuffing it into his pockets. Pia followed, scooping rings, brooches and bracelets into the brocade bag. MacFarlane raised his eyes as she passed in front of him. Her face was blank. As if she were drugged, he thought. Yet she made each move with planned certainty. He mouthed a silent insult.

Anstey reached over MacFarlane's shoulder, taking the four thousand dollars without a word. The music stopped suddenly. Sarah Whitaker's breathing was hurried. Farther round the table a woman started laughing hysterically. Anstey went to the far wall. He fumbled behind the tapestry till he found the control panel, replaced the needle and turned up the volume. He stood at the end of the table, his face in the shadow.

"I want you to come here one by one. You'll keep your hands above your head. When you reach me, get down on the floor on your stomach. We'll go round the table clockwise." He pointed the gun barrel at Whitaker. "You first."

Pia handed him half a dozen rolls of wide surgical tape. He knelt down, pinioning Whitaker's wrists and ankles —

hitching the man's arms in the small of his back. Anstey rolled him over. Using Whitaker's handkerchief, he taped it into his mouth. The gun in Pia's hand held the rest of them steady.

"Anyone with false teeth take 'em out," instructed Anstey. "We can't have you choking to death."

One after another, they came from the table to be trussed and gagged. Sam Slade was out of his faint. He stumbled across, a beautifully made set of false teeth in his fingers.

"I've *got* teeth," Anstey said with contempt. "Get your hands over your head!" He put his arms round Slade's bound body and propped him against the wall.

It was MacFarlane's turn. Biceps pressing flat against his ears he started toward Anstey. He said nothing. There was nothing to say.

"Put your hands flat against the wall," Anstey instructed. "And keep 'em up." He drove a doubled fist into MacFarlane's back, finding the kidney. "Come on — you've seen a gangster movie!"

His eyes were too bright. Never for a second did he lose his wide smile.

Sarah Whitaker came last, walking round the table, looking her hatred. Her lopsided face was streaked with make-up. As she reached Anstey, she covered her mouth with a hand, speaking with difficulty. "You vile brute!"

Anstey took a step nearer. He slashed the bridgework from her hand with a sudden movement. Then he pushed his gun against her throat. "You think hard if you want to keep on living. I'll kill you without any regret," he promised. "Where's the rest of your jewelry kept?"

She answered in a whisper, her eyes closed tight. "In a safe in the bathroom."

"And the key?"

She shook like an epileptic. "In my dressing table. The top righthand drawer."

He forced her down on the floor, ripping her skirt as he wrenched her ankles together. He stuffed a handkerchief in her mouth, breathing heavily as he stood up.

"You know where her bedroom is," he said to MacFarlane. "Let's go. Put your arms down and act naturally." He jammed the snout of the gun under MacFarlane's shoulder blade.

Anstey took one last look round the room. Pia stood by the fireplace, her gun trained on the grotesque array of bound bodies. "Will you be all right?" She nodded.

MacFarlane watched her warily. Every move she made was an economical acceptance of the situation. That nerveless calm belonged to a professional — either that or she was shocked beyond showing fear. The gun prodded his back. Both men paused in the silent hall. Behind closed doors, the music continued to play quietly. He led the way up the soft-lighted staircase. The Whitakers occupied the whole of the second floor. Beyond that, stairs led to the guest room he had slept in. The servants' wing was a hundred yards from the main body of the house, isolated by a covered passage.

He turned the flowered handle on the white-painted door. Inside the room was warm and scented. A lilac-colored lamp burned on the dressing table. The yellow and gray curtains were drawn. Silk canopies swept from above the wide bed to its carved head. Their feet made no sound in the yielding carpet as they crossed to the dressing table.

He stood in front of the mirror, watching Anstey's face.

"Open the drawer," ordered Anstey. It slid out easily.

Piled stockings were under his hand, each pair sealed in its cellophane wrapper. He hesitated till the gun barrel dug in, bruising his back. He groped beneath the stockings, finding the long slender key.

Anstey opened the door to the bathroom, jerking his head. Inside the heat was oppressive. MacFarlane waited uncertainly, the key in his fingers. Anstey tapped along the side of the tinted bath, the walls. There was no sign of a safe. Over the make-up table a mirror was set in the warm tiles. He ran his fingers carefully down to its edge. Grunting satisfaction, he swung the glass outward. The steel face of the safe had been painted to match the tiles.

"Open it up!" said Anstey. His mouth was a narrow line of concentration, the persistent smile gone.

The key turned easily in the lock. A slim writing case lay across the top shelf. Beneath it a square jewelry box. Reaching past MacFarlane, Anstey snapped the catches. The jewels nestled in suede-padded layers. They flashed in the light as the Englishman transferred them to his pockets. He locked the safe, tossing the key on the table. He took MacFarlane's hands — pressing the fingers firmly against the polished surround of the lock.

He stepped back, letting his breath go. "Behave yourself on the way down. That's all you've got to do — behave yourself."

They waited on the landing. Nothing moved in the hall below. The drawing room was as they had left it. The one light blazing over the green baize — the muted music — the trussed bodies on the floor. As Anstey shut the door, Pia came toward them. She looked past MacFarlane. He saw the gun shaking slightly in her hand.

"OK," Anstey said quietly. "Now let's get out of here!" He ripped the tape from Sarah Whitaker's mouth. Dragged her sagging body to the house phone. He bent over her.

"Now think!" he urged. "You want to get in touch with your chauffeur — using this. What do you do?" She looked up at him her lips moving soundlessly. "Think!" he insisted. "The sooner we're out of it, the sooner all this is over."

"You dial . . ." she made an effort. "You dial five."

He spun the circle. A voice answered and he held the mouthpiece close to her, whispering his instructions.

"Eugène?" Her voice quavered. "This is Mrs. Whitaker. Tell Bates I want the big car at the front door in five minutes." She faltered. Anstey prodded her. "Some guests are leaving for Cannes."

Anstey cradled the receiver. "Good girl." He used the torn strip from her dress to gag her.

MacFarlane's arms were beginning to ache. He shifted his feet, peeping into the mirror. Pia was standing behind him, her gun pointing at his shoulders. He lowered his head on his arms, unwilling to see her masklike face. Anstey left the slit in the curtains with the sound of wheels on the gravel outside. He took one last look at the recumbent figures then pocketed his gun. One hand hidden in his jacket pocket emphasized his command.

"MacFarlane — you come with us."

Lowering his arms, MacFarlane followed the pair to the door. Pia's gun was in her bag. The hall was still quiet, the front door closed. There was no sign of a servant. Mac-

Farlane licked his bottom lip. If Bates rang the bell, he thought desperately. He kept his eyes on the pass door to the servants' quarters, ears straining for the sound of footsteps. He had no plan — just hope. No bell rang.

Anstey was close behind, his voice a loud whisper. "Before we start — do you want to go on living like the rest of us?"

Not daring to move either arm or leg, MacFarlane nodded.

"All right. You're going to walk out of the front door first. I'll be behind you. Everything you do or say has got to look absolutely natural. Tell the chauffeur we're going back to Cannes. Say Pia's ill." He shoved the flat of a hand in MacFarlane's back. "It's up to you not to make me nervous," he said viciously. "Because whatever happens, you're too near to miss!"

The big door swung open easily. Bates was waiting at the bottom of the steps. His cheerful cockney voice sounded unnaturally loud after the hush of the hall.

"'ere we are, sir!" His peaked face was guileless in the moonlight. "What happened, they break you early tonight, sir?"

The door clicked behind him. MacFarlane shivered. They were a thousand meters up and the night air cold. "This lady's not well. You'd better get us back to Cannes in a hurry."

The chauffeur held the car door open, clucking solicitously. "I hope it's nothing serious, is it, miss?" Pia was first in. Bates tucked the mohair rug round her legs. "There's a doctor in Cannes if you need one. 'im that the family goes to."

MacFarlane settled in the back of the car. Anstey sat on his left. The gun barrel in the Englishman's pocket made an unpleasant bulge in MacFarlane's side. He answered for Pia.

"Just bed, Bates, in a hurry. That's all she needs — no doctor."

The car reversed in front of the lighted garages. A group of waiting chauffeurs stood drinking coffee, steam from their mugs rising in the thin air. MacFarlane strained forward, willing a sudden burst of alarm from the curtained windows on their right. But the chauffers' heads were incurious as the Rolls turned into the tree-lined avenue.

Anstey shut the last inch of the glass division. "Sit on your hands," he whispered.

The same man at the lodge gate let them out. The Rolls took the Grasse highway, gathering speed. MacFarlane found his voice. "What kind of louse are you, Anstey!"

Anstey leaned forward, watching the highway. "Tell him to go slower."

MacFarlane slid back the partition. "Take it a little easier, will you, Bates?" He sat back on his hands. He was unable to bring himself to look at the woman beside him. She was no longer calm — the tremor of her body was appreciable even through the rug. He looked at the Englishman covertly, hatred mounting.

Anstey was still intent on the road. He leaned forward, tapping on the glass. "Pull up, will you! I'm coming in front."

Anstey opened the door. MacFarlane's move to follow was involuntary. Ten yards and he'd be in dense cover. He looked at the woman. She was leaning back against the seat, eyes half closed. He felt the movement of her hand under the rug — saw the round snout of the gun in her lap. "Be sensible — please be sensible." They were the first words she'd spoken to him since the holdup. He looked away from her, shaking his head. "Sensible!"

There was a sudden flurry in the front of the car as Anstey took his seat. MacFarlane looked on, impotent, as the Englishman turned his gun on the chauffeur. The grin on Bates's face faded into fear. It was like watching a very old film — the action jerky and without sound. The car gathered momentum again. A hundred yards on, they turned left. The powerful headlights picked out the signpost. SPERACEDES.

They climbed the mountain road for fifteen miles, jolted off on a rough track and stopped. They were on a barren plateau overgrown with coarse broom.

Bates walked into the headlights, Anstey's gun in his back. He started taking off shoes, socks, finally his trousers. Anstey threw the clothing into the front of the car.

"Start walking!" He spun Bates, rapping the chaffeur's flank as he might have done a recalcitrant horse. The chauffeur shambled into the darkness still wearing his cap and tunic, his shirt dangling over long woolen underwear. Anstey watched, waiting with cocked head. The minutes passed. Suddenly the chauffeur's voice was raised in a bawl. "Help — HELP!"

Anstey fired into the ground at his own feet. The report sounded in a series of flattening echoes. The shouting stopped. Anstey took the wheel, sending the Rolls hurtling back toward the Grasse highway. At the signpost he turned in the direction of the Whitaker house. Five miles on, a roughly macadamed track led into the forest. He eased the car forward, cutting all the lights. Dense stands of pines were black in the moonlight. On the edge of the road logs had been stacked ready for hauling. The car rolled down, always in deeper silence and thicker timber. There was sign neither of house nor human being. At the foot of a grade, a sandy track covered with pine needles angled off to the left. A locked gate barred the way. At the side of the gate was a notice. PASSAGE INTERDIT — ELECTRICITE DE FRANCE.

Anstey used a key from his pocket to unfasten the padlock. The gate open, he drove the heavy car onto the track. He turned on his sidelights briefly, obliterating the tire marks in the sandy surface. The car's front wheels were now cushioned in thick pine needles. Refastening the gate, he cut his lights again.

He took the brake off, allowing the weight of the car to take it down the steep gradient. The plunging track curved left following the retaining wall of the reservoir. The water was still and oily under the moonlight — its expanse lost in the distant darkness.

The car stopped under a high bluff that hung thirty feet above the track. Anstey opened the glass partition.

"Get out, both of you."

MacFarlane stood at the side of the lane, the woman just out of reach. Her black velvet cloak was caught at throat and waist. The nose of the gun that peeped from its folds, unwavering. The Englishman turned the car off the track. It climbed the side of the bluff slowly, wheels slipping. There was a roar as Anstey engaged bottom gear. The heavy vehicle inched up, its gasoline tank banging on the rock. It was out of sight in the trees. They heard the bumpers forcing passage, ripping the saplings. A moment later it appeared on the bluff above them.

MacFarlane stepped back instinctively. Anstey was putting the Rolls at the water. There was a run maybe of thirty yards. The motor raced and Anstey leapt clear. The car gathered momentum, leaving the edge of the bluff with spinning wheels. It seemed to hang in the air above them, then the back of the chassis hit the reservoir wall. It teetered for a second before tipping forward into the water. Spray showered through the branches of the trees. Then all was quiet.

Anstey hurried down, skidding and breaking his fall with his hands. He stood in the lane, collecting a loose hubcap, part of a ripped fender. Standing on the white cement wall he dropped the debris into the reservoir.

Somewhere up in the woods, the harsh call of the nightjar sounded alarm. Left and right it was answered till the whole forest seemed awakened. Anstey still stood on top of the wall, his head high, listening. He vaulted down and rubbed dirt into the scarred cement. He came over to where they waited. His coat and trousers were torn. He touched Pia's arm.

"It was too heavy. If I'd known I'd have dumped it somewhere else. The Jaguar went easier." He was breathing quickly.

A car's lights shone miles away on the other side of the reservoir, high on a mountain highway. Anstey dug in the thick needles at the base of a pine. He came up holding a couple of pairs of rope-soled shoes, a flashlight covered in heavy rubber. He tossed the espadrilles to Pia. She slipped them on, taking her spike-heeled evening shoes in her hand.

They climbed in Indian file, MacFarlane in the middle. They were in a dry culvert, cobbled on sides and bottom.

Six times in twenty yards MacFarlane was down on his knees. Anstey stopped.

"Take your shoes off and get up on your feet!" He let MacFarlane pass first. The beam from the flashlight lit the way ahead. With bare soles it was easier. MacFarlane was leaning into the climb, groping after his own shadow.

"Up that bank," called Anstey. He pointed over his head and up to the right. MacFarlane hauled himself to the bottom level of a terraced clearing. Scrub vines, long past fruit-bearing, had been choked by grass now brown and dead in the moonlight. Crumbling stone banks stopped a couple of acres of arid land from dropping into the trees beneath. Two ruined buildings faced them on the top terrace. A farmhouse and sheep pen the color of the old twisted olive trees beyond them.

A stitch bent MacFarlane's body sideways. He leaned on the wall watching as Anstey made his way round the *cabanon*. His gun hugged against his stomach he circled the buildings, probing the darkness with his flashlight. Satisfied, he creaked the door open and motioned the others inside.

MacFarlane stood stock-still, eyes reacting to the complete blackness. He heard a bolt being rammed home. Then a match was struck. Anstey was bending over a kerosene lamp. Blue flame flickered as the Englishman touched match to the alcohol. Once the lamp was warmed, Anstey pumped, filling the inside of the building with soft light.

There was one large room. A balk of new timber thrust through iron hasps fastened the door from the inside. The two windows were hung with burlap — fresh straw covered the dirt floor. A ladder under a hatch offered uncertain access to the loft.

Anstey hung the lamp on a hook. "Put your shoes on again if you want to. You're home!"

MacFarlane obeyed automatically. The climb had left him with a dull ache under his breastbone. He started pulling on his socks, taking stock of his surroundings. Three camp beds were pushed against the outer wall. The far end of the room was a jumble of provisions, cooking utensils, a primus stove. Field glasses, radio, a repeating rifle. Next to Anstey's suitcases, a couple of motor scooters were propped against the stained whitewash. Beside them a container of fuel. Both machines were of the same make, old and travel-worn. One bore Spanish registration — the other a GB plate.

Anstey waved invitation. The barred door seemed to have restored his bluff humor. "Take a good look round." He jerked his head up at the loft. "The roof's a possible way out but I don't advise it — I'd hear you!"

MacFarlane turned his back. Till then the impression of violence and treachery had numbed any sense of personal danger. Now he was afraid. Pia was changing her clothes. She fished in one of the suitcases, standing half naked, indifferent to his regard. Her tanned face was almost Mexican in its gravity. She pulled on a neutral-colored sweater — a pair of ski pants.

He sat on the camp bed, lowering his head. The shame of showing fear was an imperishable memory — his father's study, divorced from whatever warmth and humanity might be found in the rest of the house. Unheated even in the cruel cold of a northern Ontario winter. He remembered the tall bookcase where he had straddled, holding its edge with tightly gripped hands. Through the glass at eye level were the volumes of sermons — the sterner philosophies —

63

the *Collected Works* of Sir Walter Scott. The ignominy of tears was not far away though the first stroke of the broad leather belt had not yet fallen. His father's voice, sonorous with grief and exultation.

"Aye, Neil, laddie — it's through punishment that we must all learn, here on earth." Pain stung as leather cut into bare behind. "But it's better to suffer *here*" — swish — the voice was triumphant — "than to suffer the eternal punishment of Hell!"

He made no move as Anstey came toward him. "Let's see what you've got in your pockets," the Englishman said easily. "You're the only one I didn't search up there, come to think of it. At least I knew how much cash *you* had." He laughed at his own humor and stepped into MacFarlane's reach almost contemptuously.

"What about guns — are *they* part of a gentleman gambler's equipment?" He tapped expertly under MacFarlane's armpits. Without waiting for an answer, he rummaged the pockets. He cocked his head at MacFarlane's passport. "You carry it with you now, do you — I should have known you'd be the sort who'd learn by experience." He took the document under the lamp. "No occupation — that's reasonable — Professional Gambler's hardly reassuring." He flipped a page. "The picture's not you at your winsome best, you know."

He threw the passport on the bed. Foraging in one of the suitcases, he came up holding a pair of handcuffs in each hand. He bent down, trying the steel grips on MacFarlane's ankles. They snapped shut.

"Put your hands behind your back!"

A second click secured MacFarlane's wrists. He stumbled

to the nearest bed under pressure of Anstey's hand. Three inches of loose chain governed the length of his steps.

Anstey was humming monotonously. He stopped suddenly, talking to MacFarlane. "You realize that I've got to get rid of you. The question is how. It suits my book to have the police looking for three people — not two. But eventually you become a problem." He started pacing the room, making his turns with precision. "What would you do in my place?" he asked carelessly.

MacFarlane was fascinated by the movement of Anstey's feet. Six steps right, turn. Six steps left. The length of a cell, he thought with sudden understanding. Behind Anstey's facetiousness lay danger. For the moment, the Englishman seemed content to play on his fear. There was no way of telling how long it might last. MacFarlane sensed Anstey's purpose. The Englishman would kill in his own good time. The fight to avoid it must be decided by intelligence — there was no other weapon.

Pia was paying no attention to either man. She busied herself with canned milk and water, heating the pan on the primus stove. MacFarlane looked up at Anstey.

"Give me a cigarette!"

Anstey interrupted his pacing to put a cigarette in Mac-Farlane's mouth. He lit it. "You probably fancy yourself as a man of courage. I'd forget all that sort of thing if I were you. I've no intention of letting you get away from here. You're far too important to me."

The kerosene lamp hissed in the silence. MacFarlane propped himself up on fettered hands. He blew the ash from his cigarette awkwardly. Somehow he had to shake this man's confidence. It bordered on mania.

"You really think you're going to get away with this?"

"I *know* I am." Anstey smiled.

MacFarlane nursed the stuck paper free from his lip. "The people you've robbed are going to react violently. Whitaker will just about shake the local authorities apart. Every cop'll have your description and the chance at a fat reward. I give you two days — outside."

Pia was suddenly still at her chores. She was watching Anstey who lolled on his bed. Hands behind his head. He sounded amused. "Carry on — you've got a lively imagination."

"That could be. You should try using your own a little more," said MacFarlane. "I've seen the French police at work. You won't get by a frontier. They'll search every inch between the coast and the Whitakers' house." The voiced hope gave him heart. "The sort of people you've robbed tonight demand protection. They'll get it. You've just thumbed your nose at an industry, Anstey. For my money, you haven't got a chance."

The Englishman stretched lazily. "I've seen your judgment at work and I'm not impressed. Perhaps I ought to tell you something. Sarah Whitaker was right enough. She's seen me a dozen times before. In Rome — St. Moritz — here. I've followed her across Europe. But I could never get a foot inside her house. Then you came along."

He undid MacFarlane's wrists, gave him a mug of steaming coffee that Pia carried. He seemed determined to continue his monologue.

"I could tell you more about this reservoir — the surrounding district — than the people who built it. Capacity, flow, maintenance. They're very obliging at the French Consulate

66

in Rome — even on the end of a phone. The wheelhouse is five miles away. Somebody tells the man there when to open a sluice gate. They bring his food up. And he never moves a hundred yards from the dam." He warmed his hands round his mug. "There's a routine inspection of the walls, four times a year. Fine — I've got enough food to hang on here for three months. And no water problem. Get yourself ready for bed. You can sleep on the thought!" He swallowed the last of his coffee.

MacFarlane slipped off his jacket and shirt. Anstey threw him a blanket. He handcuffed MacFarlane's left hand to the bed.

"Only the one wrist, this time! If you walk, the bed goes with you!" He dragged his own cot near Pia's and extinguished the light.

The darkness was complete. MacFarlane lay as he was. Hearing at first no more than the sound of his cautious breathing. If he lived, there could be days like this ahead. Weeks maybe. Chained to a bed or tottering round this room powerless to help himself.

Anstey had set the scene accurately. The hue and cry would be out for three people, not two. He remembered the hostility in Whitaker's denunciation. For the cops it was all too pat. They'd check back to the moment when he had first met the Whitakers. Move on to the hotel. The story of the unpaid bill and his sudden affluence would lose nothing told by the night manager. There wasn't a single step he'd taken these last two days that couldn't be turned into circumstantial evidence. Yet surely the police would listen to the truth.

He turned on his side cautiously, pushing down the

blanket with his free hand. Sound of steady breathing came from the darkness. He groped past his fettered wrist till his fingers found the smooth steel of the D ring — the loose weight of the three connecting links. The second cuff was clipped to the horizontal strut of the bed. It must slide if he moved his left wrist. He tried, holding the links carefully. His hand traveled no more than inches, stopped by the leg of the bed.

The beam of light caught him hunched over one side of the cot. He eased himself down, pulling the blanket up to cover his body. He lay quite still as the flashlight flickered the length and breadth of the cot — the windows, the door.

Anstey's voice was thick with sleep. "You bastard!" He yawned, the bed creaking under his weight. The light rested on the Canadian's head. "Sit up!"

MacFarlane struggled up, squinting into the light. He saw no more than the hand holding the automatic. He watched the index finger bend then tighten — shut his eyes and ears against the shot that had to come.

Anstey wasted no words. "Get down in your bed and stay there!"

He had no memory of sleep. No more than an eternity of waiting for day to come. He opened his eyes, searching for the familiar shapes of the hotel bedroom. The sacking had been pulled back from one window, letting in the shuttered morning. He turned over slowly. The blankets on Pia's bed were folded — she herself gone. Anstey stood in checked underpants, scraping his cheeks in front of a shaving mirror. He was humming a hymn. When he had wiped his face dry, he emptied the contents of a bottle on his handkerchief. He started working the dye into the roots of his hair with care. Patch after patch, he went at it expertly till the blond hair was completely black. Still chanting, he pulled on baggy flannel trousers, an opennecked shirt and sports jacket. The opening door did nothing to disturb his imperturbability.

Pia was neat-hipped in the elastic ski pants. Her hair was bound in a scarf. Though she passed near enough to MacFarlane's bed to touch him, she neither looked at him nor spoke.

"I'm ready for tea," said Anstey cheerfully. He ducked his head, presenting his handiwork. "How's it look?"

She inspected the dye, frowning. She wiped behind his ears with a handkerchief. Anstey knuckled his jawline, thoughtfully. "I've got to know what our friend is up to." He tested the struts on MacFarlane's bed, grinning. "He ought to have a bell on him." He swung round. "That's it — a bell!" He dropped a couple of pebbles in an empty milk can, fastened it to MacFarlane's leg irons. He threw the door open. "Now I can hear you! You've got five minutes to commune with nature. Don't go beyond the olive grove. I'll be waiting here for you."

He followed MacFarlane to the clearing, squatted on the wall at the back of the *cabanon* using his field glasses. MacFarlane shuffled into the olive grove, the can clanking as he walked. The sky overhead was black and ominous. Daylight only accentuated the complete isolation of the place. The holding had been hacked from the wooded slope — concealed almost from the road bordering the reservoir. Beyond the pinetops, the water stretched toward mountains tumbling into the far distance. He hitched up his trousers and hobbled back to the house. Rain had

69

started to fall, pattering on the fallen leaves. A hundred yards below, a solitary fig tree marked the spot where they had climbed from the culvert. Four or five miles through the forest, the Draguignan highway would be lively with traffic at this hour. But here was forbidden territory — a generation away from actuality.

Anstey was at the end of the top terrace, using his field glasses. Hearing the chink of the cuffs, he walked over — dyed hair a glossy black.

"That's the drill every morning. If you get caught short, say so!"

He leaned against the window, looking up at the sky. Dried leaves blew among cobwebs on the sill behind him. He kicked open the door. "We're going to get rain."

This time he cuffed the Canadian's wrists in front of him. Changed hair and shabby clothes had given Anstey an air of genteel seediness. He dropped the handcuff keys in his jacket pocket.

"I'll leave you like that so you can eat." He jerked a shoulder. "You can please yourself — behave or eat your food from the floor like a dog." He was rubbing his jawline, looking at MacFarlane thoughtfully. "What would you do?" he asked suddenly. "Suppose I took these things off and turned you loose?" The woman at the end of the room was quite still. Anstey waited for an answer, clicking his fingernails — his face grave.

MacFarlane watched him guardedly. The ambivalence of Anstey's behavior — his fantasy — everything added to the growing certainty in MacFarlane's mind. The Englishman was crazy.

"You've left me no choice," answered MacFarlane.

In spite of his sturdiness, Anstey was nimble in every

movement. He vaulted his own bed to sit beside MacFarlane. The cot rocked under his laughter. He was suddenly
serious. He tapped MacFarlane's leg, speaking softly.
"You'd try and run for it, wouldn't you? I'm a moderate
man, MacFarlane. But I've got a lot at stake." His nostrils
flared as he looked up at the woman. "Food," he said happily.

She fed each man impartially. A plate of egg, butter,
biscuits. A mug of hot tea. The shaving mirror hung where
Anstey had left it. She stood there, tying and retying her
scarf till Anstey exploded.

"For Crissakes! Sit down quietly and eat your food."

She carried her plate to her cot — sat staring at her lap.

"Don't shout at me, Paul. I'm sorry — I can't be like you.
I'm afraid!"

Anstey mopped up the last of his egg and put his mug
on the floor. He considered them both. "So you're afraid,
are you! Afraid of *what!* I've just pulled off the biggest
coup of its kind in years — I don't make mistakes, Pia, do
I?" She made no answer and he shouted. *"Do I?"*

She shook her head. "Please, Paul!"

Anstey jerked a thumb at MacFarlane. "Don't let him
get you rattled. He's got more to be afraid of than you have."
He stretched out lazily, catching the back of MacFarlane's
neck, digging into the nerve centers. "You're afraid, aren't
you, Mac?" One last flathanded shove rocked the Canadian's
head. "Come on — we'll do you up properly."

MacFarlane bent down, fighting the pain in his neck.
He held out his arms behind him. The cuffs snapped shut.
Anstey nodded at the small pile of books on the floor.

"If you get bored, you can always read. Get Pia to turn
the pages for you!" He put on thick-framed spectacles,

standing before the mirror to study the effect. He spoke over his shoulder. "There's a good selection — *The Jeweler's Manual — Highways and Byways of Old Provence.* No good?" His voice was almost kindly. "I'm reading *Alice* myself."

MacFarlane rubbed his stubbled chin on his shirtfront. His head had cleared. Outside heavy rain had started to fall, drumming into the hard ground in front of the house. He watched covertly as Pia made up her face. The hand holding the lipstick was shaking.

Anstey stood at the far end of the room, fiddling with the small radio. He frowned, turning the set in different directions. He looked at his watch, still maneuvering the control.

The announcer's voice was metallic. "This is Radio Monte Carlo! Here are five minutes of the latest news. Today the Chief of State . . ." Anstey signaled silence. The voice crackled on. "A robbery took place late last night on the property of M. and Mme. Whitaker, British subjects well known in the Var. Three gangsters, known to be foreigners, robbed a private gaming party at pistol point. The thieves made their escape in an automobile belonging to the victims. The total value of property involved is as yet unknown. However it is thought likely to exceed eighty million francs. Roadblocks have been set up throughout the area — police at all frontier posts are maintaining a strict watch for the fugitives. With the assistance of Interpol, an early arrest is anticipated. Meanwhile in Algeria . . ."

Anstey put the radio down. He turned his cuffs back.

"Eighty millions — sixty thousand pounds! Open the suitcase, Pia. Let's see if they're right."

She opened the locked bag — threw Anstey the dinner jacket he had worn, her brocade bag. The Englishman draped the coat across his knees, emptying each pocket methodically. He counted, smoothing the crumbled bills with stubby fingers.

"Thirty-six thousand, four hundred seventy-five dollars." He snapped a rubber band round the roll. "Twenty-nine thousand Swiss francs." Another rubber band. "And a hundred and sixty quid in fivers. Not enough French francs to bother about." He pushed the money across the blanket. "Put all this back, Pia. Before it gives this rogue ideas!"

He emptied the brocade bag in his lap, telling her to light the lamp. He held the pile of jewels in both hands, turning them so that a hundred facets flashed response. Using a large magnifying glass, he inspected each piece in turn. Once he fastened a square-cut emerald on his little finger, admiring the beauty of its setting. Each trinket was wrapped in twists of face tissue — the whole padded in cotton and laid in a small wooden box. He made a neat package, closing the ends of the paper with sealing wax. He was droning his dirge as he printed the address in block capitals.

Pia turned from the window where she had been standing. She picked the straw flecking her sweater with nervous fingers.

"It's after ten. You said I had to go outside then. I'd see nothing in this weather."

Anstey carried the misted binoculars to the window — sighted on the end of the clearing — the gate on the reservoir road. He threw the glasses back on the bed.

"You're right! Not a thing! Just beautiful solid sheets

73

of rain! By this afternoon, there won't be a cop within five miles."

Pia folded her blankets again, unnecessarily. "I don't want to be left here alone, Paul."

Anstey stretched out. He started cleaning the two automatics, the repeating rifle. "You'll do as you're told," he said at last. He broke open a package of shells, sniffing the powder on the back of his hand suspiciously. He was paying no attention to either of the others.

Water dripped to the floor from the loft. MacFarlane's eyes found the source. Light showed through the tiles in the roof. If they ever left him alone, it was a chance. Handicapped as he was, he could butt his way through the tiles where the roof sloped. The twenty feet drop would have to be risked.

Pia was reading. The tension showed in the set of her mouth. What shock she had aroused in MacFarlane left him angry rather than revolted. The naïve intimacies of yesterday were a ridiculous memory. He hauled himself up, stretching his legs awkwardly.

"I'm getting cramp — is it all right with you if I walk a little?" He stumbled toward the end wall and Anstey.

The Englishman brought the rifle to his shoulder with one smooth movement. He sighted along the barrel, clicking the empty magazine repeatedly. For a second MacFarlane stopped then moved on doggedly. He made his turn slowly. The package of jewelry was on the foot of Anstey's bed. Anstey's voice was sardonic. He used the butt of the rifle to push the package nearer MacFarlane.

"Read it! Go ahead — read it out loud!"

MacFarlane obeyed. "Monsieur William Spicer. Poste

Restante, Annecy." Annecy was close to the Swiss frontier. He looked up at the Englishman. "I think you're getting worried. Why do you have to convince me how smart you are?" He waited at the end of Anstey's bed, watching for some sort of reaction.

Anstey wiped the bridge of his nose. "I don't think I'm worried," he said mildly. "It's an odd thing — there was a moment when I was going to put this deal to you just as it stood. Then I decided you were a mug — and I don't like mugs." He pulled a blue-covered folder from his pocket. "You've seen a British passport, of course. Listen to this — William Spicer, Master Printer. That's *me!*" He put the document away, smiling broadly. "It's even got my picture on it. You're wondering why I should tell you all this. It's simple. You're not going to get the chance to use any of it against me. I don't *like* people like you, MacFarlane. You're neither one thing nor the other. You'll slobber over a woman like Sarah Whitaker so you can trim the rest of those mugs there. You'll gamble with anything except your liberty. And that makes you honest!" Without saying anything else, he went through the door.

MacFarlane floundered back toward his own cot. Pia was watching him from the window. "Could I get a drink?" he asked.

She stood for a moment undecided. Then, dipping a mug in the water pail, she held it to his lips. He drank till the water ran down his chin to his shirt.

Her eyes were still vigilant. She put the mug back in place, speaking hurriedly.

"You're not being very sensible. It's dangerous to taunt Paul. Can't you see that?"

75

A trace of her scent reminded him of a time too long ago. The Casino bar — the hotel terrace, quiet in moonlit morning.

"He's not right in the head," MacFarlane said suddenly. "You're too scared of him to admit it." His feet jingled as he stood up. "You heard what he said — he's going to kill me. What do *you* do when the time comes — hide your head?"

Her hands hung loose by her sides, her eyes were half shut. She spoke with sincerity. "Half these things he doesn't mean — he's only dangerous when he's frightened."

"You think so! Look — he's spelling out every move for me. Why?"

She peered through the shutters at the driving rain. She suddenly turned, facing him. "Every time he tells you something, he reassures himself. There's no other reason. When we go from here, you'll be left — alive."

He looked round the room. "Left to rot — that's even better."

She shook her head. "I promise you it won't be like that. You're full of hate, Neil. For him — for me. Please don't make it so obvious!"

He had the impression she was about to say more. But she went back to the window. Something other than fear bound her to Anstey. A link he must discover to break it. "You started using me the minute we met," he said bitterly. "I never asked who you were — what you did. I don't even know that it would have made any difference. What's the matter — were you ashamed of being his lover?"

She flushed under her tan. "I wasn't lying. He was my lover — a long time ago."

He shut out the thought of Anstey's mouth on hers —
the blunt fingers caressing her body. "Then what's the hold
he's got over you — do you know what it's like in a French
jail, Pia?"

"I know what it's like in a Spanish prison." She was very
straight. She shook the memory from her. "I shall never
go back."

It was an act of faith. Anstey's insensate confidence
seemed to have enveloped her. MacFarlane looked at her
incredulously. "What's that supposed to mean — that you'd
rather kill yourself?"

Her voice was without emotion. "That's what it means."

He hobbled across the room. She moved away, keeping
her distance. "Then *why* . . ." he started. "I don't believe
a word of it. I've got to help you, Pia. Don't make it too
difficult."

She spoke with restraint. "You can help me by not anger-
ing Paul. It's too late for anything else."

They sat in silence till Anstey rapped on the door. He
came in, swinging the rain from his cap. He stood as if
gauging the feel of the room with some extra sense. "What's
the matter?" he asked softly. "Did I come back too soon?"
Neither answered. He tipped across the room, moving on the
balls of his feet. Pia's eyes were shut as her face lifted
under his hand. He let her go suddenly, his voice easy.
"I've been as far as the gate." He stripped, rubbing himself
dry. His voice was muffled behind the towel. "What's our
guest been saying, Pia?" The top half of his head showed.
He was smiling.

She took the damp towel — hung it on the end of her
cot.

"Shall I get the food ready, now?"

He nodded. "It's never too soon for me as you know."
He was humming again as he walked to the steps to the
loft. He set a pail under the leak. A lunge of his foot brought
the ladder to the ground. The rotten wood broke in a dozen
places. He came across to MacFarlane, dabbing behind
his ears where the dye had run. "Silence worries me — let's
talk." He sat down looking at MacFarlane's cuffs. Taking
his automatic, he rapped the butt against the handcuff lock.
Steel bit into MacFarlane's wrists. He held them steady,
digging his heels in the straw.

Anstey leaned back. "In the old days you could spring
them — you know, rap 'em on a cell floor or something.
They make them differently now." He heaved up, scratch-
ing his back against the wall. "Try to imagine the police
are after you! They *are,* come to think of it! All right —
you hear on the news that Interpol's after you. Are you
worried?"

MacFarlane answered cautiously, resolved to humor the
other.

"I'm worried."

Anstey followed a crack in the ceiling with the point of
his gun. "Ah, but Interpol."

MacFarlane shrugged. "I heard. That's worse, isn't it?"

The reply pleased Anstey. He smiled happily. "You see,
even the smart gambler's impressed by newspaper talk. They
build up this picture of Inspector Whatnot, immaculately
dressed — probably speaking five languages. A super sleuth
hanging round airport terminals. And waiting for me. The
truth is that Interpol's nothing more than an office. An
international clearing house for information. There isn't a

working cop among them. And when the police *have* no information, they can't exchange it." His voice was languid. "Has Pia told you she's half Spanish, not Italian?"

His tone tripped warning in MacFarlane's mind. Anstey's insistent confidence troubled him in spite of the woman's assurance. He took a deliberate risk. "She told me nothing. On the other hand, you're telling me too much!"

Anstey swung his feet from the bed — found the familiar path from wall to wall. Pia was preparing the meal, her back turned to them.

Anstey came to a halt. "I've told you I don't like your type, MacFarlane. But I want peace. You remember your carols, no doubt. Peace on earth and good will toward men. I may not even kill you. It's possible that I'll leave you here for the police to find. They want to see you as much as they do me. You'd be better off thinking up a story that they'll believe. Take my advice and stay clear of the truth!"

MacFarlane considered the possibilities. Anstey's sinister pose could be an affectation. He hadn't seen inside the passport the Englishman had shown him. The scooters, escape route — the business with the parcel of jewelry — all of it could be staged to cover Anstey's real plans. A convincing performance that MacFarlane would be left to reproduce for the police. The hope died. It was too tortuous. The alternative carried more weight. Anstey intended leaving a dead witness behind — not a living one.

The Englishman wrapped a cloth round a can of beans, puncturing it carefully. He poured the contents over a plate of frankfurters and gave it to MacFarlane. "Good grub — eat while you can!"

He sat on his own bed, eating as he listened to the radio. The music stopped — the announcer's voice was portentous.

"Violent storms hit the length of the Mediterranean littoral this morning. In Nice, sea lashed the Promenade des Anglais, uprooting street lamps. At the Palais des Festivals in Cannes, water invaded the orchestra pit, the first four rows of fauteuils. *Electricité de France* announces an abnormal flow into the Peyroud Reservoir. Measures have been taken to keep the level within safety limits."

Anstey finished his food, looking at his watch. He spoke to Pia. "I'll give it till four — this weather, it'll be almost dark by then. The post office in Grasse doesn't close till six. There'll be plenty of time." He screwed up his face, mimicking her. "I thought we'd settled this long ago. I'm going and that's the end of it. Wherever the police are looking, it won't be in this area now."

She kept her head down, rinsing the dirty plates. "I don't want to be left alone, Paul."

"It isn't a question of what you want," he said quietly. "The sooner that parcel's on its way the better." He went to the door — flung it open. An east wind had freshened, driving great sheets of rain scudding across the clearing. The mountains beyond the reservoir were lost in banked black clouds. He shut the door. Picking up the volume of *Alice in Wonderland,* he carried it to the window. He read sedulously — chuckling as he turned the pages.

MacFarlane was quiet on his cot in the half-light. Outside the rain beat steadily. The livening wind sent a loose shutter clanking against the wall over his head. Pia dragged her cot to the far end of the room. She sprawled, her arms hiding her head.

Suddenly the even drone of an aircraft insisted through the weather. A high-pitched roar that neither gained nor lost in intensity. Anstey was first to react, moving crabwise to the door, head turned as he listened. He peered out into the rain. As MacFarlane watched, a helicopter flew in over the pinetops. A giant dragonfly that hovered in the storm. It came in low above the farmhouse. It was near enough to make out the open cabin door — the figure of the man leaning from it. The noise from overhead was thunderous. Losing vertical height, the craft drifted down toward the reservoir.

Anstey's indecision lasted only seconds. As he ran for the rifle, a second motor clattered — this time from the direction of the road. The wind carried the sound of men shouting. Then all was quiet. Anstey closed and barred the door at speed. He ran the length of the room giving Pia instructions. He threw her an automatic — stacked boxes of ammunition on the sill. Putting his arms under MacFarlane's bed, he dragged it from the window.

He pumped a shell into firing position, speaking over his shoulder. "A word out of you and you've had it!"

Pia was standing flat against the wall, breathing noisily. Anstey snarled a warning. "Keep that bloody sniffle under control!"

From where he lay, MacFarlane was able to see through the chink in the window. Anstey leaned forward, his gun coming slowly to the ready. A man was climbing from the culvert at the end of the clearing. He stood, peering uncertainly into the rain. He started up to the top row of terracing. Anstey's elbows splayed as he trained the rifle on the advancing man's chest. Twenty yards from the house the stranger stopped. He scooped the water from his neck with the side of his hand. Then he walked across to the sheep shelter, disappearing behind the walls.

Pia coughed, strangling the sound with her hands. Anstey moved impatiently, his weapon steady. It was five minutes before the stranger reappeared. A couple of salvaged planks were balanced on his shoulder. Managing them with difficulty, he lowered himself back into the culvert.

Anstey put his mouth close to Pia's ear. She nodded, looking down at the automatic in her hand. The Englishman had the door open again. Holding the rifle at the port, he skidded down the muddy terracing.

MacFarlane moved cautiously on his bed. Pia stood halfway between him and the door. He lowered his legs to the ground. Her voice was without compromise.

"Keep where you are!"

He balled his shoulders. "What are we going to do — wait for them to come up and get us?"

Light filtered through the shutters on the side of her face. Strain etched a line from nose to mouth — the skin was tinted with fatigue. "Don't move, Neil," she repeated.

He had his head bent, gauging the chances of a flying tackle. He heard her retreat in the direction of the door — almost as if she had read his mind. His voice was flat.

"Do you think they're visitors? It's the police, Pia!"

Anstey was back on the run, careless of noise. He leaned against the closed door, taking in the scene. It was barely possible to hear what Pia said.

Anstey's shadow grew long on the wall. He stood over MacFarlane, rain running down his face. Suddenly he dug his fingers into MacFarlane's neckband. He hauled the Canadian upright to stand tottering on shackled feet. "Did you tell her it was the police?"

The clenched knuckles bruised MacFarlane's thyroid. He pushed feebly against the steady pressure. Just as suddenly, Anstey let him go. He fell backwards, his hands up to protect his throat.

Anstey wrapped an arm round the woman. "I told you — watch this bastard. He's out to rattle you if you give him the chance. It's nothing — there's a bit of the reservoir wall gone. They've been plugging it. The helicopter was inspecting the dam."

She broke free — ran past MacFarlane's bed to throw herself on her cot. Anstey watched moodily as she burst into tears.

He turned to MacFarlane with savage sarcasm. "The Old World gallantry's wearing a bit thin — the handkissing and the rest." He spoke to the woman impatiently. "For Crissakes pull yourself together!"

She struggled up. Expressionless she used her hand mirror. Anstey took off his jacket. He wrung out the sleeves, dirty water oozing through his fingers. "Those people down there will be finished in half an hour. I'll follow them out." He lit the lamp, hanging his jacket where it might dry. Wheeling the scooter to the center of the room, he propped it up.

She was touching and retouching her mouth with lipstick. She shut the bag, speaking with decision. "If you're going into Grasse, Paul, I must come too. You can't leave me here alone."

Anstey was straddling his machine, his voice deceptively patient. The swollen vein in his forehead disclosed his anger. "We've talked this out fifty times, Pia. You're going to stay here and watch him!"

He stowed the package of jewelry in a saddlebag. She

said nothing. "Let's have a look at your gun." He checked the magazine and mechanism and returned it to her. "You can forget the modesty. If he wants to go outside, you go too. Don't lose sight of him. If you have to use your gun — try to get him in the leg. But *get* him!"

She was holding his oilskins in her arms. She parted with each piece reluctantly. "I've got a feeling about this, Paul. Please wait! In a couple of days it will be safe — but not now."

Anstey gave his machine careful attention, checking fuel, brakes and tire pressure. He sat in the saddle, considering her.

"If I'd listened to you, I'd still be under lock and key." He turned his wrist. "A quarter to five. I'll be back at nine, the latest." He shrugged. "If not, do the best you can for yourself. I won't be in any position to help you." He wheeled the scooter to the door. She took down the bar for him. He touched her face with gloved hand, his eyes bright for MacFarlane. "Now *watch* him!" he warned. He looked at the hanging jacket. "Don't let that coat burn — it's the only one I've got to wear."

She stood till she could no longer see him. Then shutting the door she went to her cot. For a while she sat picking the edge of the blanket. She lit a cigarette and blew smoke at the wall in silence.

MacFarlane watched her guardedly. He had too little time to save them both — manacled and faced with a woman determined on destroying herself. He spoke on impulse.

"You've got to listen, Pia. We haven't got much time. If you'll do what I tell you, we've got a chance. *You've* got a chance!" He held out his wrists. "Take these things off!"

She crossed the room to stand at the window. The whine of the scooter sounded through the battering rain. She was holding the automatic steadily.

"I can't."

He sought an argument that might convince her. "We've got to get in touch with the police. These people are human. I'll swear you went into this business in fear of your life. I won't leave you," he urged. "Wherever they take you, I'll be there!"

The small gun lifted to point at his stomach. "You're wasting your time. I did nothing in fear of my life."

He dropped back on his bed hopelessly. "Do you know what a psychopath is?" Something in her alertness drove him on. "Can't you realize that this man's insane? You're either going to follow a maniac or finish in a ditch with a hole in your head. Is that it?"

She sat on the extreme edge of her cot, her face impassive. "I lived too long with those words to be impressed. Whatever he is, they made him. You ask a lot of questions. Let me ask you one. Hasn't there ever been anyone in your life who needed you?"

He answered with sincerity. "I think you do."

She moved her head impatiently. "Suppose I told you that I'm still in love with Paul — would you believe that?"

He shut out the last vestige of jealousy with deliberation. "I'd try to."

Her mouth was bitter. "I used to go to visit him once a week — for three years it lasted. The Pendennis Center for

Mental Healing — it sounds so innocent, doesn't it? Most of the time he was in a strait jacket. He always knew me. I signed his committal papers."

For the first time he felt near her — with a truth he could accept. His tone was gentler.

"If it hadn't been you it would have been someone else. What matters is that he's crazy now. The best way of helping a mad dog is putting it out of circulation."

Her dark eyes leveled. "You talk precisely as the military doctors did — only even more brutally. Oh, I've heard all the arguments — 'twenty million men came out of the war the better for the experience' ! I don't believe it! Paul was a hero at nineteen." She shook her head. "It's too young."

He shrugged. "That gives him license to act like a thug for the rest of his life?"

She answered him with patience. "It gave him the need to go on feeling important. I've been conscious of it since the first day I met him. Even with you he's playing a part. All the gangster's talk — the pose of being the great jewel thief. He never stole a penny in his life till last night." She stared as if willing him to believe her.

He was doubtful — unwilling to credit that Anstey's obsession could carry him to such lengths without experience. "How've the pair of you lived?" he asked suddenly. "The four thousand dollars he produced were real enough."

Her voice was proud. "On money I earned and saved. He ran away from that place a year ago. I was in Rome working. He found me there."

She threw him a pack of cigarettes, matches, returning to her end of the room as if determined to keep distance between them. He lay awkwardly on his chest, propping his chin on manacled hands.

"What about you and that business of going to jail in Spain — was that true?"

Her head lifted defiantly. "Yes, it was true."

"Would you tell me what happened?"

She used the end of one cigarette to light another. "I stole a woman's jewelry. And I was caught. It's not a very interesting story."

"It is to me," he insisted. "There's got to be a reason."

She made him wait. "Isn't it enough that I did it?" she said at last.

"For the police, maybe — the judge. Not for me!"

Her face across the room was in shadow. Her laugh an unhappy attempt at indifference. "I was governess to a very rich family — people like your Whitakers. I needed money for something. There is your reason."

The jumbled pieces were suddenly clear in his mind. "For Anstey?"

She stopped him. "No more for him than for me. For our marriage. It didn't matter. I had a baby in prison. She died at birth. When they let me go, Paul and I were married." She stared at him for a long time. "I am glad the baby died."

The need to know was indefatigable. "Are you still married to him, Pia?"

"No. We were divorced four years ago. I hadn't seen him for a long time before he escaped. What else do you want me to say — isn't it enough that I went back to him!" The way she said it was a complete acceptance of fact.

He had a quick sense of outrage at her perversity. Memory took him to the frame church — the fat stove clanking by the family pew. His father, gaunt and accusing from the pulpit . . .

". . . a blind and obstinate love of the devil! As long as we cherish the spirit of unrepentance it shall be our undoing!"

. . . the can rattled as he swung his legs to the floor.

"You're sick," he said with feeling. "As sick in the mind as he is. The man's a criminal lunatic — you owe him nothing. Can't you think of yourself for once!"

She looked up, speaking very quietly. "Can *you?*"

He sat with lowered head, irresolute. She needed his help. Till he was able to give it to her she must be treated as a jailer to be overpowered at the first opportunity. Overhead the rain drummed the roof, an incessant reminder of passing time.

It seemed that an hour went by like that, captor and captive alike silent and afraid. She still chain-smoked, going to the window to listen — coming back to sit with gun cradled on her knees.

She spoke to him at last, her voice friendly. "Talk to me, Neil. Tell me what it's like to live as a gambler." Her smile was rueful. "I'm sick if I lose a thousand francs. I think most women are like that — they live too close to reality. Hasn't there ever been anyone you loved who tried to break you of it?"

He eased the cuffs. Already there were raw patches on his wristbones. Once again she'd maneuvered him into intimacy. And what was there to tell . . . the dreary sequence of chance meetings through the years. The mutual boredom that ended each venture — leaving him with the dream un-

88

shared. Imagination painted it in different colors but the base was always the same. A house with land where his kids might grow up among horses. A dozen times he'd had the money to turn the dream to reality. The woman never.

"Somebody called gambling 'the quality that gives substance to daydreams,'" he said. "It's near enough, I guess. I never tried to explain — I just accepted the urge. As I do now." He lifted his cuffed hands. "It's just three days since we met, Pia. But you're my responsibility. That's a gamble, too. You can't always apply reason to living."

She stood under the lamp, turning Anstey's drying jacket. He heard the chink of keys at the same time as she did. She felt in the jacket pocket. He made no move as she dropped the handcuff keys into her own pocket. She went back to her bed.

"I can't believe it all," he said suddenly. "What made you pick on me?"

She spoke through a haze of tobacco smoke. "Two days ago on the beach, I wanted to tell you to go — never to see either of us again. Oh — I knew what Paul was going to do." She moved restlessly. "But I was lonely like you. Happy enough, I suppose, to be wanted. Now I'm ashamed."

He dragged deep on his butt. "If you even had a chance in all this. How long do you think he'll last in Grasse? These people aren't fools — they'll be looking for any foreigners roughly the same build and height as all of us. They'll throw them in jail first and ask questions afterwards."

Her gesture was a complete denial. "He'll come back."

The gun was still by her side. If he tried for the keys, despair could force her to use it. He kept talking, trying for words that would lull her suspicions.

"You said it on the beach — Cannes was full of women. I had to pick you."

Her smile mocked him. "You're a romantic, Neil. Look at me — I'm not one of your good and innocent girls. I'm a thief!"

He turned away nervously. She was still able to shock him — to strip his thinking of pretense. What she said was true. But he thought of the thieves he'd met in the crowded paddocks. The poker schools in sleazy basement joints. The thieves he knew carried their reputations with touchy bravado as she did — or hid behind unassailable and respectable fronts. You gambled with them, giving or taking money without an exchange of references. It had always seemed simple enough to adhere to society's rules. Bucking them was a stupidity. Only the troubled in spirit had time for nobler motives.

He waited till the stub burned itself out on the floor. "I can't watch you follow a man like that for the rest of your life — not without doing something about it."

She crossed the room to pour more oil in the lamp. The new soft light gave her face serenity. "There's nothing you can do, Neil. Nothing!"

She was three feet away, the gun on the floor where she had knelt. He made his play, hobbling toward her. As he neared she groped for the automatic.

He held out his hands. "You don't need that," he said steadily. "I'll play the game you want but let's you and me do it the right way."

She came to her feet, leaving the gun on the ground. He took the hand she gave him, twisting it in the small of her back. As he forced her down, she kicked wildly. He hitched her arm still higher.

"Drop the keys to the floor!"

The steel ring fell in the straw at his feet. He dropped his hands to her waist, drawing the gun nearer till his weight rested on it. He pushed her from him violently, shouldering off her nail-raking charge as best he could. It seemed a lifetime before he was able to fit the key to his handcuffs. Next came his ankles. He shoved the gun in his pocket with a shaking hand.

She struggled up beside the bed, her eyes bitter. He bent over her and she spat full in his face.

"*Cabròn!*"

He held her arms, crushing his mouth against hers. Breaking away, she backed to the wall, wiping her mouth. He vaulted her bed, beating her to the loaded rifle. She was at the door, struggling with the bar. He went toward her slowly, soothing as he might have done a nervous animal.

"I don't need this gun, Pia. You know it. You're coming with me if I have to drag you every yard."

Her head drooped against the bar. "He'll kill you and I'll be glad of it!"

He stopped at the window. "We're going to the police, Pia. Together!"

It seemed an effort for her to speak. "If you meant any of the things you said, you'll make a bargain. I'll do whatever you want — go where you tell me — if you'll help me."

He was filled with sudden suspicion. "What sort of bargain?"

Her fingers crept up under his cuff. "Wait here till Paul comes back. Let them have the jewelry — the money. Don't you see — you're the master now. You can give him your orders. Only give him a chance before you go to the police. The chance he gave you."

91

He dragged his hand away, his voice incredulous. "The chance he gave *me* — you're insane!"

"You're still alive," she reminded. "He'll kill himself rather than be taken. Explain why you're letting him go free — make your conditions. But let him go. You're not a policeman, Neil. What can it matter to you? If you do this, I'll come with you gladly."

He heard what she said with misgiving. She had no qualms about turning Anstey loose — her fanatical devotion held no reason. For a second he had the idea of giving it to her straight — Anstey was better off dead. Her dark eager eyes betrayed him. The idea of a pact with her was strangely exciting.

"He'd sacrifice you to save himself — and never give it a thought," he said.

She nodded. "I have no illusions about Paul."

As he looked at her, the solution was suddenly clear in his mind. So obvious that all along it had eluded him. It was the Whitakers he must reach and not the police. Once Anstey returned, anything that had been stolen would be under his control. He could bargain its restitution against his freedom and Pia's. French law made it as easy to call off a prosecution as to institute one. He had no doubt what Sarah Whitaker would do. She'd see a hundred people go free in order to retrieve what had been stolen from her. The surging confidence gave him new life.

He looked down at Pia. "It sounds a one-sided bargain. How do I know you'll keep your end of it?" He had no qualms about the deception. His only anxiety now was for Anstey's return. He wanted the Englishman back with either the jewelry or what stood in its place.

92

She twisted her hair in a bun on her neck. "I shall give you proof," she said.

His mood changed. In spite of himself he was unable to trust her completely. There could be some sort of signal arranged against the event. Some way in which she might warn Anstey to stay clear of the house — leaving him at large with a gun he'd be ready to use.

"Don't think I've got any illusions about you either," he said. "The only thing that matters in your life is that bastard's safety. I'd like to see him back where he belongs. Either that or dead. What'll he do when he leaves here — who'll be next on the list — or doesn't any of that mean anything to you?"

She was fixing her face. Her mouth was redder — softer. The room was sharp with her scent. "I know what the end must be for someone like Paul. But I must try to prevent it."

"I'll let him run. What time is it?"

She barely raised her sleeve, fishing a fresh pack of cigarettes from her bag. "A little after ten."

He dragged her fingers from the face of the watch. It was past eleven. His voice was hot with sudden doubt.

"What are you lying for?"

She answered him hesitantly. "I was afraid that you'd want to go. What do you think's happened to him, Neil?"

"I don't know." He was wondering. Instinct prompted him to leave. The Whitaker house was ten miles away — his route planned. The highway was too dangerous. He had as much interest now in avoiding the police as Anstey. He'd go over the gate at the end of the track — into the woods at the east end of the valley. Most of the way

93

would be ankle-deep in slush. It could be daylight before they made it. Yet without the jewelry or the paper controlling it, the journey would be useless.

He let go her wrist. "Do you know how to pray?"

She shook her head. "Not any more."

His voice was harsh. "We'll try! If he doesn't get back, we've all had it!"

She stood with lowered head, irresolute. Then with sudden movement she kicked off her rope-soled shoes. As he watched, she removed her clothes. For a second her body gleamed honey-yellow in the lamplight. She got into his bed without a word, pulling the covers to her chin. Her hand moved on the rough blanket.

He propped the rifle against the wall, looking down at her. Then lay down beside her. Passion obliterated the ache in his body. He took her with no thought beyond surcease.

Time passed. His shoulder was pillowing her head. The scented smoothness of her hair against his mouth. The lamp sizzled on the far wall — the monotony of rain on roof an invitation to doze. He was keeping his eyes open with effort.

Disturbed by a sound outside, he sat up. The shutters over their heads had definitely moved. He raised himself up cautiously, keeping to one side of the window frame.

Anstey was standing there looking into the room. Lamplight slit the shutters, striking on the Englishman's wet face. He disappeared suddenly into the darkness, leaving whatever he shouted lost in the wind.

MacFarlane fastened the heavy screens with trembling hands. He threw Pia's clothes on the bed and grabbed the rifle. All the frustrating uncertainty of the past two days was gone. He had to go out and hunt Anstey. His first thought was for the lamp. He turned the screw and the light died. His last impression was of Pia's tense face. He groped his way toward the bed to hold her trembling body.

"It's Anstey. I've got to go out there."

Her fingers were digging into his arm. The whisper was hopeless. "Did he see?"

He held her still tighter. "You're going to open the door. Shut it again immediately but leave the bar down."

He felt for her hands, folded them round the butt of the automatic. He led her to the door and unfastened the bar an inch at a time. He stood the balk of timber against the wall.

"I'm going through the window. When you hear me say 'right,' you open the door then slam it shut. Then get under the bed and stay there!"

He ran to the shutters, easing them inward. Shinning up on the sill, he crouched there. As he called to her, he heard the door open. With its slam, he pushed his feet outside and let himself drop. There was no sound from the house. Nothing but rain that pelted into the mud where he lay. He wormed away from the door, holding flashlight and rifle clear of the slush. Visibility was nil. The pattering gutter overhead his only guide. He crawled on, mud invading his clothing with every move. He went as far as the sheep pen on his belly. Each outward thrust of his hands a reminder that Anstey might be on the end of it.

The lee of the pen was sloping ground. He came up slowly facing the house beyond the crumbling wall. Save for the olive trees behind the *cabanon* there was no other cover nearer than the watercourse. He felt his way inside the

95

shelter. The ancient sickly smell of sheep surrounded him. And something else. He sniffed the faint burned fumes. Then his leg struck against metal. Fingers explored the outline of Anstey's scooter — the hot motor casing. The saddlebag was empty.

In spite of his soaked body, his mouth was dry. He ran outside. Holding the flash well away from him, he thumbed the button. The powerful beam cut through the rain to the olive trees.

"Anstey!" he shouted. "I've got the rifle! Come into the light with your hands over your head!"

He put the flash on the top of the wall, training it on the culvert. A yard away, he lay low, the rifle ready in his hands. A choked drain gurgled behind him. There was no sign of Anstey.

He waited for seconds then cut the light. Vaulting the wall, he ran back to the house. The sudden tug on his ankle took him in mid-stride. He fell forward, the rifle smacking into the mud.

Anstey jumped up from where he had been lying. The butt of his automatic caught MacFarlane over the ear. He was still conscious as Anstey dragged him feet-first into the *cabanon*.

The Englishman charged the darkened room like a bull. "Light the lamp, you whore!" he shouted.

A spluttering match showed Pia's face as she bent down. She straightened up, hanging the lamp on its hook. Anstey walked delicately now. He stopped in front of her. Then using the flat of his hand, he struck her across the face.

"Whore!" he repeated. Rage and wounded vanity made

his mouth ugly. He whipped round, throwing oilskins on the bed. The 6.35 was almost hidden in his palm. He tossed the gun after his clothing.

"Get up!" he told the Canadian. "I'll do this with my hands!"

MacFarlane lay gulping in the sweet wet air that blew through the open doorway. He got to his feet as slowly as possible. Blocking the first vicious swing, he drove his knee at Anstey's groin. It caught the swerving Englishman's hipbone. Anstey was moving quickly, hands held low and boring in. He hooked hard at MacFarlane's stomach, grunting as the Canadian's left split his lip.

MacFarlane backed toward the wall. He was outweighed and outpowered. He flicked twice with his left again — found Anstey's head with a solid counterpunch. Anstey still came forward, spitting blood from his mouth. He took three — four — blows on the way in. Wrapping his arms round MacFarlane's body, he bent the Canadian backwards.

Agony spread from MacFarlane's loins, flooding the strained lumbar muscles. He let himself go limp. Anstey's grip never faltered. He was breathing heavily, head tucked down, using his weight as a lever to break MacFarlane's back.

The sound of the shot was deafening. The stink of burned powder filled the room. MacFarlane staggered against the wall. Anstey looked at his right hand in amazement. The last two fingers were shattered. The woman had shot from close range. Anstey was muttering to himself. Suddenly his voice was clear. "Not *you*, Pia!" He lifted his arm with disbelief.

Her eyes were strained but she held the gun steadily.
"Search him, Neil!"

MacFarlane emptied the other's pockets. Passport, operator's license, a few thousand francs. Anstey's face hardened
as MacFarlane opened the passport case. Inside was a small
yellow slip. A receipt for a registered package. Destination,
William Spicer, Poste Restante, Annecy. MacFarlane pocketed it — tossed the rest of the Englishman's property back
at him. He took Anstey's gun from the bed.

"Hold him there!" he said to her.

The rifle lay in the mud outside. Taking the barrel in
both hands, he swung the butt against the wall with all
his force. Again and again till metal split from wood. He
went back to the house.

Anstey was wrapping his hand in the dressing Pia had
given him. She turned as MacFarlane appeared.

Her voice was tired. "Tell him what he has to do, Neil!"

MacFarlane spoke without emotion. "Our bargain's finished, Pia!"

She ran across the room to him. "It can't be!"

"It is," he said steadily. "I'll let him go. You leave with
him or with me. But it's got to be your own choice."

Her voice was quiet but definite. "I want him to go free.
And I never want to see him again."

In spite of himself, he was fascinated by the Englishman's
lack of fear. "You heard her!"

Anstey's right hand was a bloody bundle. He nodded.
"How long have I got?"

"Till daylight." MacFarlane forced the top suitcase with
a tire lever. He counted out four thousand dollars —
wrapped the rest of the money in one of Anstey's shirts. He
spoke to the Englishman. "I don't know whose this is,

yours or hers. But she's not going to need it any more!"

Anstey pocketed the bills with his good hand. "It happens all the time," he said slowly. "So long, Pia!" For the moment he was the man of two days ago. Bluff, frank and confident. He wrapped himself in his oilskins, stopping at the door. "So long, MacFarlane. Till we meet again!"

They heard him squelching up the wooded slope behind the house. MacFarlane spoke gently. "Pia — we've got to go!"

She nodded, fighting for composure. "Now I'm really afraid. He'll never let up."

"You don't have to be afraid — not any more," he promised. One pledge had been fulfilled. He accepted the implications of a greater trust. He glanced at her feet with misgiving. On a night like this, the rope scandals were useless. "Haven't you got any other shoes?" He wrapped himself in the jacket Anstey had left. "Passport?"

She nodded. "I have only the shoes I wore last night." The short suede coat buttoned to her throat, her hands were pushed deep in the pockets, the shape of the gun she'd used plain through the soft green leather. Her look for him held new diffidence — the tone of her voice was compliant. "Where are you taking me, Neil — to the police?"

He put out the lamp for the last time — took her arm. "Forget the police — just trust me, Pia. That's all — trust me."

He led her into the rain. They crouched by the stone bank. Water coursed down the face of the granite blocks. He wrenched a couple of them free. The earth inside was dry, protected by a thickness of turf. He pushed the bundle of money as far as he could, replacing the stones. Then packed mud into the crevices.

They slithered down the terracing to the culvert. Drains had burst on the surrounding slopes, charging the gulley beyond capacity. He lowered her into the torrent. They went down, slipping on cobbles they could no longer see. Thirty yards on, he dragged her from the culvert. Hand on the back of the slippery leather jacket, he propelled her into the trees. His head had cleared completely, the cold drenching rain giving him fresh power. Ever since he had the post-office receipt in his possession, one thing had occupied his mind. She must never know that Anstey was to be a deliberate sacrifice. He had to stop her being present at the interview with the Whitakers. He felt her slowing. She came to a halt against a tree, holding it with both hands. "My feet." She lifted a leg, He groped past the ankle. The sodden canvas had been trodden under her heel — the rope sole twisted. He stripped off the espadrilles, kneading back the circulation to her feet. "Get into my shoes," he insisted.

She wouldn't stay the distance. He had to find a place to leave her. Somewhere she could rest till he came back sure of their safety. As yet they'd gone no more than five hundred yards from the *cabanon*. "Give me your hand," he urged. "We've got to go on."

Wet pine needles sank under his bare soles. Stumbling, they made their way down to the lane skirting the reservoir. The other side of the concrete wall, the lake boiled under the downpour. He helped her over the gate. The hard-top road was awash with debris rushing down the slope. To the right it climbed to the Grasse highway. To the left lay unknown territory — a direction that must take them away from the Whitakers' house.

He started up the grade, pulling her after him. Her head was lowered into the rain, the end of each breath a gasping complaint. He climbed doggedly, her hand locked in his. More than ever, he sensed her dependence — finding new determination in the thought. At the top of the hill he halted, steering her to the edge of the road. They had to go east soon — the main highway could not be far away.

He half walked, half fell to the stack of cut timber. His numbed feet were no longer reporting pain or cold. They sat there for a while surrounded by black and inimical darkness. The forests he remembered were friendly. Places where you lay in your bag at night, the smell of the dying fire good in your nostrils. Around you, the rest of the crew wrapped like cocoons. There were sounds but they were comfortable sounds. The sudden cackle of a loon — the rustle of maple leaves dislodged by the passage of bird or animal.

He turned up the collar of his jacket, shivering. Her hands were icy. He breathed on them, feeling the shake of her body as she whispered, "I don't think I can go much farther."

The end of the journey was always clear in his mind. He held her wet face close. "We'll find some place where you can rest up," he promised. "Daylight's only a few hours away."

Her grip tightened painfully on his shoulder. "You're not going to leave me, Neil?"

He took off her shoes, wringing out her socks again. He tied the shoelaces tighter. "Another couple of miles. There'll be somewhere to shelter."

A motorcycle roared to a stop far too near. He pushed

her down in the mud, rolling behind the log after her. A man's voice called. MacFarlane brought his mouth close to her ear.

"Stay here. Don't move!"

He wriggled in the direction of the voice, propelling himself on his stomach. Twenty yards on, he heard the sound of conversation — the rapid French incomprehensible. Two men were standing on the highway. It had been nearer than he thought. He wormed his way to the left. Stood behind a tree listening. The men had stopped talking. He moved forward cautiously. The sudden plunge of a ditch took him by surprise. He slipped down, gasping as the water reached his waist. For a second he crouched there — then brought his head up slowly. The men were fifteen yards away — the glow of their cigarettes marking their position. It was just possible to make out the rounded helmets of motorized policemen.

He backed up the ditch, keeping his face to them, fighting the swirling water. They were watching the highway — not the road to the reservoir. The junction of ways made a perfect vantage point. He dug his fingers deep in the mud, hauling himself from the ditch. He crawled back to the log pile, his face close to the ground.

She was lying as he had left her. Before she could move, he had his hand over her mouth. He lifted her to her feet. She walked unsteadily under his guiding arm. They shuffled into the trees and away from the highway. The pattern of their going was unchanging. Underfoot the squelch of mud and pine needles. Tripping over raw roots denuded of earth by the pressure of water. They jogged down the slope, brambles tearing at their clothing. Suddenly his bare feet trod on asphalt again. He stopped, bending double to ease the stitch in his side. They were in a lane following the course of an ancient gulley. A tall stone wall made one side, retaining the terraced earth above. On the other, the bank rose to the forest they had left.

He took toeholds in the wall and pulled himself up. A grove of cypresses ringed the house on the hill. No lights showed there. Clambering down, he urged her along the track. They followed the telephone wires overhead for a hundred yards. A five-barred gate blocked their passage. The latch gave under his pressure — the gate opening and shutting without protest.

They were standing in a driveway that circled past the cypresses in the direction of the hidden house. To their right, outbuildings straggled into a rough-fenced paddock. Galvanized-iron roofs creaked in the wind. He walked over to the garage. A propped stone held the doors shut. He hauled it away — pulled Pia in after him. He felt his way along the side of the car to the door handle. The interior was warm and smelled faintly of cigar smoke. A rug was spread across the wide front seat, protecting the upholstery. He draped it round her shoulders. She leaned back, her body relaxing.

A clock ticked on the dash. He tried the buttons in front of him. Raw cement blocks glittered in the blaze of headlights. They were sitting in a large American convertible. His first thought was for the ignition keys. The chromed lock was bare. He cut the headlights. It was still possible to see in the soft glow of the parking lights. The keys didn't matter. With roadblocks out on the highway, stealing a car achieved nothing.

103

The clock showed a quarter to three. By seven it would be light enough for the police to stage a full-scale drive across the countryside — if ever Anstey broke cover. Mac-Farlane knew he had to get to the Whitakers before the police took the initiative. He took her hands gently. "How do you feel?"

She opened her eyes, her head barely moving. "This time it's true, Neil. I can't go any farther."

His hands explored the interior of the car, the deep door pockets. Maps — a few garage bills — a round metal disk holding an out-of-date British license tag.

He lifted her legs up on the seat. A cushion from behind made her a pillow. He covered her body completely with the rug. "I want you to listen to me, darling." Dark eyes were following every movement he made. "I've got to leave you here for a bit. But when I come back it'll be with a car that will take us both into Cannes." She was looking at him without understanding. "Look — you've got to trust me, Pia. I can't tell you now but I've got the answer. We're both going free."

Speech seemed an effort for her. "How long will you be?"

"Not long," he said steadily. "I'll be back before daylight with any sort of luck. It doesn't really matter — you'll be safe enough as long as you do what I tell you." He held up the British license — the garage bills — for her to see. "The people who live here are English. If you hear them moving about before I get back, show yourself. Only remember this — you don't speak any French or English. All you can say is this — 'telephone the Whitaker house.'" He repeated the words. "Nothing else." He pulled her upright, pressing his mouth on hers. "Will you do that, Pia?"

She struggled her arms free of the rug, caught in some sudden fear. "What are you going to the Whitaker house for?"

His lips touched her cheek. "There's no time to explain. I'm going and I'll be back."

She huddled back beneath the rug. "Those men on the road — was it the police?" He nodded.

"Looking for Paul?"

He shrugged. "I doubt it. If they are, it's all vague enough. Nobody knows where he is."

Her voice was hesitant. "What'll he do, Neil? Do you think he has a chance?"

He lied as best he could. "He's got the same chance he always had. I'm going, Pia. Will you do as I've told you?"

She lay still, looking up at him. "You're not going to lock me up in here — I couldn't bear it."

He shook his head — put out the sidelights. "Give me a couple of hours — time enough to get to the Whitakers. If I'm not back then and you're scared, show yourself to the people here. Goodbye, Pia."

Her hand found his in the darkness. "Goodbye, Neil!"

He left the garage door as he had found it. Running across the square yard, he took the driveway curling up to the house. Slipping from cover of the cypresses to a flagged path that meandered up to a silent loggia. His bare feet were quiet on the tiles. The low rambling house was built on two levels. Lights flickered through the open window in front of him. He peered in. Chintz-covered armchairs flanked a wide chimney where the remains of a woodfire still burned. He tiptoed back to the path. These were people who lived without suspicion. They'd phone the Whitakers before the police.

Passing the outbuildings at the bottom of the driveway, he heard a shod horse scrape on cement. He opened the bottom half of the hinged door, stepping into the warmth of the stable. The horse blew hard, moving its hindquarters away from him. He kept flat against the wall, talking softly to the animal. Moving toward its head, he felt his way past the empty hay net. He stayed for a while, his hand on the soft muzzle, letting the horse smell him.

A fodder room was next the stable. He opened it up and found the light switch. There were no windows. He dragged a sack of oats across the bottom of the door, blocking any leakage of light. A second door in the far wall gave access to a harness room smelling of oiled leather. A variety of bits and bridles hung from hooks in the beam. A couple of saddles perched on trees.

He searched his memory for the right equipment. A snaffle bit, the plain English saddle. A heap of clothing lay on top of a wooden case. Corduroy trousers, an old pair of flying boots, a thick wool shirt spiked with hayseeds. He changed his clothes, leaving the wet garments on the packing case. First he stole a man's horse, he thought, then his clothes. Events finally making a thief of him. His brother's voice sounded, pompous with the knowledge of one year at law school. "If you take this book from me, Neil, with intent to permanently deprive me of it, *that's* stealing!"

Maybe the owner would see it that way. Already his body was warming in the heavy flannel shirt, his feet regaining feeling in the lined boots. He needed a light to saddle up. He dragged the sack of oats from the door. Taking a halter with him he led back the horse. The chestnut stallion stood quiet, head on arched neck almost snakelike as it sniffed the sacked grain. It had been years since he'd put a bridle on a horse. He held the straps awkwardly in one hand, feeling for the animal's gums with the other. It took time before he maneuvered the nickel bit into the horse's mouth. He was warm enough to sweat now, his skin sensitive to every hayseed sticking in the shirt. He threw the saddle over the chestnut's back. As he tightened the girth, the head came round, open-jawed. He rapped the animal's muzzle, ramming home the buckle.

The stallion followed him into the yard without fuss. A simple bar let them into the paddock. He picked his way across rough sodden turf, leading the horse to the far side of the field. This was going to be a whole lot different from the tanbarked riding school — the short breezes through the park on some hired hack. This much was sure — the chestnut would always see better than he could in the dark. All he had to do was stay in the saddle and keep the animal headed in the right direction.

A stone wall marked the beginning of the encroaching trees — too high to negotiate. He looked back at the house. No lights — no noise. A gate a few yards on opened to a path into the woods. The trail led due east in the direction of the Whitaker house. He left the gate open behind him.

A foot in the stirrup took the weight of his body. The horse moved forward as he swung into the saddle. Almost unconsciously, he gripped with his knees. The chestnut responded, stretching into a canter. MacFarlane ducked his head, taking the driving rain on the side of his face. The sense of speed was exaggerated in the darkness — the horse's hoofs thudding into the soft going. The saddle seemed pitifully small — he bumped awkwardly, striving to keep his balance.

He eased his grip on the reins and the stallion's stride lengthened into a gallop. MacFarlane was leaning forward, knees clutching desperately, his hand going with the movement of the horse. A sweep in the trees ahead warning of the bend. The chestnut took fresh hold on the bit, ears twitching. It rounded the curve with gathered speed.

The reins were gone. He twisted cold fingers into the long mane, shoving his heels well home in the stirrups. His face was pressed hard against the horse's wet neck. Helpless in the saddle, he galloped this way for a couple of miles. Suddenly the pace slowed. He grabbed the swinging reins with stiffening fingers. He bent forward, turning his wrists, getting a firm grip on the animal's mouth.

The chestnut picked its way down a slope loose with shale, blowing hard. MacFarlane wanted to dismount. If he did, he knew he would never get back in the saddle. He kicked his feet out of the stirrups, bending over the stallion's neck, ready to swing himself free. They slithered down, the film unrolling in his head. The massed charge of twenty steeplechasers as they met the first fence. The flying hoofs of horses twisting in mid-air — the jockeys left on the ground. A horse would always try to avoid a fallen rider — that's what they said.

He clutched as the chestnut's hindquarters heaved. Its hoofs struck the rocky ground in an effort to regain traction. They stopped at the bottom of the hill. He soothed the animal mechanically, his own fear thudding in his chest. The smell of the horse's sweat was acrid. He sat up straight in the saddle, clucking encouragement.

The stallion took the slope easily. The earth was drier there. Deep running ditches kept the trail free of water. They covered five miles over level going till the track swung sharply to the right. Headlights came and went beyond the bend. They had reached the highway again. He put the horse at the trees in front of him. A couple of hundred yards on, a high wall curved in both directions. It was the end of the line.

He dropped to the ground and unsaddled. As he unfastened the throat lash, the chestnut's ears came forward, easing its head from the bridle. It nickered softly. He dropped the harness at the base of the wall then swung his hand hard at the animal's flank. He heard it hammering back down the trail toward its stable.

He leaned against the wall, sick with exhaustion. Muscles he had forgotten were stiff and aching. He tried gauging his position. The Whitaker's gate lodge would be about a half mile along the highway toward Draguignan. He followed the wall, looking for a way of scaling it. An old scabbed pine thrust out a branch that he climbed. He dropped down on Whitaker property.

He thrashed through the undergrowth, careless now of the noise he was making. Suddenly he heard a dog bay. He crouched at the foot of a tree, protecting his throat and face with his arms. A Doberman charged from the wet darkness, the impact of its surge knocking MacFarlane free of his hold. He rolled on the ground, the dog's weight on his back. The muzzled jaws were close to his neck, the animal's growl terrifyingly near.

A flashlight illuminated the scene — a man's voice sounded, sharp with command. The dog retreated. Mac-

Farlane climbed up, blinking into the light. He was breathing hard, his labored French scarcely understandable. He came forward, walking slowly, his hands above his head.

"Take me to Madame Whitaker!"

"*Reste-là!*" the man said brusquely. He snapped a chain on the dog's collar then lifted his shotgun, holding MacFarlane at bay.

The automatic MacFarlane had taken from Anstey was still in his trouser pocket. He tossed it at the guard's feet.

"I am a prisoner," he said. "Take me to Madame Whitaker."

His quick movement had brought the dog to the end of its chain, snarling. The guard retrieved the weapon and held a whistle to his mouth. He sounded three blasts. A few seconds passed — another guard came pounding through the trees toward them. He was tall, drenched, and handled his dog with savage authority. There was a rapid interchange in patois. The second man loped across to Mac-Farlane while his companion held the light steady. The tall one ran his hands briefly over MacFarlane's body. The gold in his mouth glinted.

"*Marches!*"

His outthrust hand sent MacFarlane staggering. They moved off through the trees. Beyond waterlogged lawns, the house lay quiet. The only lights burning were in the far end of the servants wing. They marched toward it, stopping in a yard at the rear of the garages. The tall man threw open a door.

Olive wood smoldered in the rough open fireplace. It was a large bare room, whitewashed to dazzling cleanliness. Benches flanked a scrubbed dining table. A coffeepot bubbled on a smaller table against the wall. Beside it was an incongruous telephone.

MacFarlane sat on the cane-bottomed chair, gripping its sides. The tall guard had taken the dog to the kennel at the end of the yard. His voice was loud as he silenced the yelping. He came back to lean against the closed door, his shoulders almost covering the width of the panels. Head and coloring were Moorish. He flicked the rain from his cap, studying MacFarlane.

"*Tu parles français?*" he asked curiously.

MacFarlane nodded. He raised the cuffs of his corduroy trousers. The skin round his ankles was raw and suppurating.

"I've been a prisoner." He pointed at the phone. "I want to speak to Madame Whitaker!"

The tall guard's eyes might never have known sleep. He belched, coming over to inspect MacFarlane's wrists and ankles more closely. He lit a cigarette, throwing the pack on the table in front of the Canadian. He said something to his comrade.

The older man's uncertainty was plain in the way he handled the telephone. He spoke his piece rapidly — replacing the receiver as though responsibility passed with the action. He poured three cups of coffee, suddenly amiable, one for MacFarlane.

Five minutes went by. The cockney chauffeur burst through the door. He was wearing a thick blue sweater over uniform trousers. His feet were in carpet slippers. He stopped dead, looking with amazement at MacFarlane. One hand caressed the single strand of gray hair across his head.

MacFarlane set his mug on the floor. Conscious of his

111

stinking body, the coarse stubble covering his face, he spoke quietly. "Hello, Bates!"

The chauffeur kept his distance, his expression wavering between fear and satisfaction. "Well, look 'oo we've got!" He circled MacFarlane cautiously. "*Mister* MacFarlane!" He tried a few words of French on the guards — his face sour with lack of understanding. "Can't make head nor tail of the buggers," he muttered. He came back to MacFarlane more happily. "It's all waiting for you, mate. Fifteen years 'ard labor! And be all accounts, them French nicks ain't no 'oliday!"

The two guards stood side by side, their heads moving as they sniffed for a lead. MacFarlane tried to give his words assurance. "Get Mrs. Whitaker on the phone — I've got to talk to her right away."

Bates's lock of gray hair wafted with the fury of his head movement. "It's the police you'll talk to, mate, not 'er!"

MacFarlane climbed up painfully, supporting himself on the back of the chair. The post-office receipt was a sudden embarrassment. If this lunatic called the police, he'd be in a cell before the Whitakers heard about it. He stared at the edge of the table, concentrating on each word. "Try to use your head, Bates. I've come here voluntarily. I've been a prisoner for two days." He looked up, his urgency dominating the chauffeur. "You'll either take that phone and call Mrs. Whitaker or lose your job and go to jail. It'll be you — not me!" He sat down heavily. The phrase rolled importantly. "Obstructing the apprehension of a felon — do you know what that means, Bates?"

The chauffeur's red face was bright with indignation.

The words seemed to revive memory of a hundred parking offenses. "I 'ain't made no obstruction!" He swung his head round. The guards' blank expressions offered no help. He swallowed, his throat bulging. "You're a crook," he said weakly.

MacFarlane'e hands hung by his sides. Guards and chauffeur stood looking uncertainly at one another. He was working the folded post-office slip between the cane chair bottom and leg. He stood up. No one stopped him as he went to the phone.

"All right — what number do I dial?"

The guards were impassive, their duty done. "Number one," the chauffeur said at last.

MacFarlane spun the dial. For a while the insistent buzz went unanswered. He replaced the receiver and dialed again. Seconds after, Sarah Whitaker's voice sounded, edgy with sleep.

"Qui est là?"

He spoke distinctly. "Neil MacFarlane." He heard her breath go. "I'm speaking from your house, Sarah. I want you to listen very carefully. If you let anybody call the police, you'll lose everything you had stolen the other night. See me and I'll help you get it back." The earpiece went dead. He waited, knowing she had a hand over the microphone.

George Whitaker's voice sounded, irate and important. "Where are you speaking from, MacFarlane?"

MacFarlane waited for Bates to tell him. "The guards' dining room," he repeated. "There's Bates here and a couple of your men." Whitaker's voice was just audible as he relayed the information to his wife. "Forget about the po-

113

lice," urged MacFarlane. "If you want your property back, get some clothes on and come down here right away!"

He waited for the reply, sweat dripping from his ribs. The heat in the room was suddenly intense — the figures of the watching men blurred. The picture of Pia as he'd left her was persistent. Her voice as she'd said goodbye. He came out of his daze to hear Whitaker repeating himself irascibly.

"What's the matter, MacFarlane — can't you hear me! Let me talk to Bates."

He gave the chauffeur the instrument — staying near enough to overhear the conversation. He had to get back to her as soon as he could — she was at the limit of her resistance.

Bates held the phone fiercely, his face composed to respect. "Yessir — no sir, in the grounds, I think. I found 'im 'ere with Edmond and Marius, sir." His head nodded vehemently. "Immediately, sir!"

The chauffeur looked the room over, hardnosed and confident. Taking the tall guard's shotgun, he tapped himself on the chest importantly. He seemed taller in his carpet slippers as he turned to MacFarlane.

"All right, mate. The guvnor's going to see you inside. And don't try any funny business — I've got me instructions!" He lunged, the shotgun held in bayoneting position. "I never fired one of these things in me life. But it can't be *that* difficult!" He followed MacFarlane into the yard, through the door into the servants' wing.

They walked into the commotion of a suddenly awakened household. Heads either scared or curious peeped from behind doors watching their entry. Bates waved them aside.

114

In the main hall he stood at pot-bellied attention, the barrel of the shotgun pressed firmly into the carpet. He stiffened as the Whitakers hurried down the stairs.

George Whitaker's clothes had been assembled at random. Black shoes — the bottom half of a tweed suit — an odd jacket. He took the last few stairs on the run — his demeanor that of a man determined to assume command of a desperate situation.

"Hold that bloody gun the right way up!"

The chauffeur reversed the arm at speed. Whitaker stopped in front of MacFarlane, buttoning his jacket. He peered at the Canadian cautiously. "Has he been searched, Bates?"

The chauffeur took a step nearer. "Yessir!"

"In the study, George!" Sarah Whitaker had done all she could in a very few minutes. Her hair was bound in a scarf — her eyes and lips cared-for. She wore her well-cut slacks and sweater with confidence.

Whitaker snapped the study lights, making for the tall chair behind the desk. He opened a drawer, scowling into it significantly. MacFarlane took a position a few feet away. Sarah Whitaker switched on a heating unit, her eyes curious. Her husband assembled his properties — telephone to the right — pen and paper in front of him. He used the paperknife like a gavel, rapping for attention.

"All right, MacFarlane, what's the story?"

MacFarlane kept his gaze steady, ignoring the man behind the desk. "What I've got to say is for the three of us, Sarah." He nodded at the heavy-draped windows. "Let's stop playing cops and robbers — I'm not going anywhere. I came here of my own accord."

The chauffeur shuffled, looking for guidance. Whitaker

115

exploded. "You bloody scoundrel! You'll give no orders here!"

MacFarlane shrugged. He chose the most comfortable chair and sank into it. "Have it the way you want," he said indifferently. "I'm trying to avoid scandal."

Sarah Whitaker came from the glowing fire, one hand restraining her husband's choler. "I find it very difficult to reconcile your attitude with your last appearance here. Are we meant to apologize for being robbed?" Her smile was inimical.

MacFarlane eased deeper in the cushions. She watched intently as he showed her the marks on his limbs. "Either we did as Anstey told us — that girl and I — or took a bullet in the head. Not that it matters what you think, but we're innocent. If you want your money and jewelry I can get it for you!"

Whitaker's face was fiery. "I'm sure you can!"

"At a price," MacFarlane added.

Whitaker blew open disgust. "Rubbish! You've come here with some cock-and-bull story. I have my own ideas why!" He stopped short under his wife's hard stare. He half rose from the chair, bellowing at the chauffeur. "Don't stand there gaping, man! Wait in the hall!"

MacFarlane waited till the door closed then hitched his chair a little closer to the woman. "Listen, Sarah. I'll put it on the line — the two of us are innocent. But if we were guilty the deal I'm offering would be exactly the same. It's our freedom against the return of the stuff that was stolen." He linked hands, stretching his arms. "I'll give you Anstey as makeweight for the police."

Whitaker slammed hard at the top of his desk. "What's

the use, Sarah! We've had this out before! The fellow's nothing but an adventurer." He seemed to take MacFarlane's calm as an outrage. "Who brought those two people into our house?" he demanded.

She was leaning back against the bookshelf. Her voice was cutting. "Your bellowing must be intriguing for the servants. I have every intention of hearing the end of this, George. If you don't want to listen, wait outside with Bates."

Whitaker's defiance dwindled to an angry mutter. "Ever since he wormed that first invitation, I've had him taped. I always told you there was something fishy about him." He rubbed his hand uncertainly over his chin — astonished to find it unshaven. "Too much the gentleman to be one," he said darkly.

It was gone six by the gilt clock over the mantel. The woman touched her headscarf, self-conscious under MacFarlane's scrutiny.

"I've left a letter behind," he said coolly. "If I don't get out of this house safely, it'll be mailed to the newspapers." He turned from one to the other, letting the import register. "I don't suppose it would prove anyone's innocence but this much is sure — if that letter gets into print it'll show your guests that *you* stopped them from getting their property back."

The clock ticked on in the hushed room. Daylight was not far off. Noise of a loose horse could easily alarm the people in the house across the woods. He had no faith in Pia's ability to face them and feared for her. There'd been no phone call as yet or Sarah Whitaker would have mentioned it.

She broke the silence. "What do you expect us to do,

Neil? The whole thing's out of our hands now. What are we supposed to say to the police?"

"I'm going to draft a statement that you'll both sign," he answered. "Your money's not too far from here. Once it's in your possession, your statement's going off by registered mail. Then you get your jewelry back." He spread his hands. "It's a simple arrangement — both sides are safeguarded."

The desk rattled with Whitaker's passion. His face grew redder. "If you believe a word of what this scoundrel says, Sarah, you're completely mad!"

She blocked a yawn, studying the movement of her neck in the mirror. "How much of this story *is* true, Neil?"

He shrugged. "All of it. If I seem to be doing things the hard way there's a reason. I've learned something this past couple of days — you don't prove yourself innocent by saying so!"

Her face was hidden as she bent over the fireplace. "The police have been here five times. They seem to know a great deal about you." She looked up, her eyes quizzical. " 'A penniless gambler' ! That's how they describe you, Neil. They say that you borrowed the money from that man to pay your hotel bill in Cannes. Is that true?"

Her insistence irritated him. Every wasted second added to Pia's uncertainty. "Sure it's true. That doesn't make me guilty of robbing your guests at pistol point." A portable typewriter stood on a table beyond the desk. They watched cautiously as he went to it. "I'm not pleading for anything," he said flatly. "I'm offering a deal. If you agree, I want five hundred dollars as well as our safety. Enough to take the pair of us out of the country." He swung round on

118

Whitaker who was licking his lips. "You're the big wheel, George. You spent a lot of time telling me how you fixed that business with your guards and the Arab they shot. OK. You shouldn't have any difficulty calling the police off now."

"Take the *pair* of you out of the country, you say!" She stood with her back to him, looking into the mirror. "Then the police are right about that, too! You're all old friends!"

"Of course they're old friends," her husband broke in. He looked at MacFarlane with the red hostile face of a child. "We'll see! The police are getting a report on you from Canada. If you ask me, even this professional gambler pose is a blind."

MacFarlane watched him somberly. "The letter I've left will be on its way at nine. Is it a deal or not?"

Whitaker rose, leaning white-knuckled on the desk. "I forbid you to have anything to do with this, Sarah!" He took the telephone. "The Procureur in Draguignan can deal with it."

She caught his wrist with an easy movement. "There's been enough trouble, George. I want our guests' property back. And my jewelry. Up to now the police haven't been able to do much about it." She was sure and commanding. "He'll sign, Neil. We'll both sign."

He carried the typewriter to the desk — found paper and carbon. He made five copies of the statement, addressing envelopes to the British, Canadian and U.S. Embassies in Paris — the French Ministry of Justice — the last to himself in care of Canada House in London. He read the document through to them carefully.

119

TO WHOM IT MAY CONCERN

WE, George and Sarah Whitaker, make this statement free of any threat and without hope of any promise. We have taken the necessary steps to withdraw charges of armed robbery proffered against Pia de Tellier and Neil MacFarlane. We do this satisfied that neither of these persons took culpable part in the theft committed in our house. Any future institution of proceedings against these two people would be malicious and without basis in fact.

Signed . . . *George Whitaker*
Signed . . . *Sarah Whitaker*

He tossed the papers on the desk and went back to his armchair. He watched them impassively, hiding his own involuntary doubt. Whitaker donned heavy reading glasses, grunting his way through the statement. He pushed the typewritten sheets across the desk to his wife.

"It's blackmail. Obvious blackmail! They're not worth the paper they're written on."

"That's a chance I've got to take," answered MacFarlane.

The woman moved impulsively. Taking the pen, she scrawled her signature on each page. She sat on the desk, tapping the statements with inkstained fingers. "You've had two days that I rather think you've enjoyed, George. All those policemen fussing about the house. And nothing's been done. Either you'll sign or be the laughingstock of everyone we know."

The pen spluttered Whitaker's grudging signature. His voice was giving him trouble. "And what about the police — the various insurance companies that are concerned! It doesn't matter, I suppose, the trouble I'll have with them!"

Sarah Whitaker fastened the typewritten sheets in their envelopes. She turned to MacFarlane, her face old with doubt.

"Forget it," he said quietly. "You'll have no trouble there. You'll be saving the insurance companies money. That's all they're concerned with. The police . . ." He shrugged. "They'll do as George tells them. If they still want a victim, they've got one." He pictured the Englishman, wet and desperate. Anstey wouldn't give up as easily as all that. There was no real reason for him to suppose that their fear of the police wouldn't be as great as his own. Likelier that he'd see himself as a man double-crossed. And he'd be back for whatever he thought belonged to him. "Don't bet good money on the cops getting Anstey," he said on impulse.

Whitaker frowned into the open telephone book. "Where do you say the fellow's hiding?"

MacFarlane hesitated. The role of police informer was still distasteful.

"Well come on!" Whitaker's logic was ponderous. "You're supposed to be innocent, aren't you? If you're innocent, it's to your advantage to have this man caught." He thumbed through the pages, looking up. "If you don't *want* him caught . . ."

"The Procureur will have to know — he's in charge of the investigation, Neil," the woman broke in. "His authority only goes as far as this department. If this man's hiding somewhere else, it means that other police will have to be informed."

He answered her slowly. "Two hours ago he was in this department. Let them do what they can with that to start."

Whitaker picked up the phone. Both voice and manner had regained their customary assurance. He spoke testily,

121

covering the mouthpiece to express indignation to his wife. "Still sleeping!" He waited, holding the crackling instrument well from his ear. Then spelled his name twice. "No, madame, his secretary will *not* do! That's right — the Procureur de la République himself. Let *me* be the best judge of that, madame!" His voice was guarded as he spoke again. He put down the phone. "Leiclier himself will be here in the hour. He's bringing officers."

Sarah Whitaker switched off the fire, her eyes enigmatic. Straightening, she turned from one man to the other. "It's absurd us staying here looking intense. We all need something to eat." MacFarlane looked down at the soft veined hand holding his sleeve. "You'd better let me see those cuts, Neil!"

Stiff-backed and hostile, Whitaker opened the door to the hall. The chauffeur shuffled nervously under his inspection.

"Get rid of that shotgun," snarled Whitaker. "And put some proper clothes on." He stopped at the foot of the stairs calling back to the chauffeur. "I want the station wagon in half an hour."

MacFarlane followed them. In front of him, Whitaker walked in silence. His bedroom door slammed behind him. His wife shrugged and led the way to her bathroom. She bent to retrieve a flimsy garment from the pink carpet. "Sit down."

He sat on the small stuffed stool. Behind him she rummaged in a medicine chest. Beyond the battery of bottles, the wall safe was half open. "I almost forgot — you've been here before!" Her voice sounded amused.

She bathed and poured iodine on his wounds, leaning closer than was necessary. She fastened the dressings.

"There!" She was looking over his shoulder into the mirror. The soft light was kind to her. "Women are always curious, Neil. Why this sudden interest in the Italian girl?"

The curtain at the window swung slightly in the breeze. Pale light was breaking from behind the dark cloud barrier. It had stopped raining. He touched the beard on his face with nervous fingers. "Could I shave, Sarah?"

She plugged an electric razor in its socket and sat on the edge of the bath watching him. "Aren't you going to answer my question?"

He hid his face in the thick towel, cheeks stinging from the cologne. "You get interested in *anyone* you've been locked up with," he mumbled. "If you both happen to be innocent, that's an additional reason."

Hands and neck made a graceful curve as she joined them. "Then perhaps I should try it," she said wryly. "Where are you going when you leave here, Neil?"

Whitaker's bellow sounded from the breakfast room. "You'd do better to ask him what he's done with my bloody car!"

She pulled down the corners of her mouth, kicking the door of the bathroom shut. She sat in front of her mirror, touching her mouth with a lipstick. "Well, where? Back to Canada?"

He leaned against the door, watching her with displeasure.

"To England," he said heavily.

She reached over her shoulder, holding out a small spray to him. He squeezed, sending a cloud of scent at the back of her hair. As he replaced the spray, her fingers caught his wrists, pulling him down. "You're a fool," she whispered.

He stood, tall in the glass, his face impassive. Her mood

changed suddenly. "You're not going to tell me you've fallen in love with her!" She swiveled on the stool, her eyes mocking him. "You can't be serious!" she challenged. "It's beside the point whether or not she's innocent — she lived with a thief — that's hardly a recommendation!"

His voice was dogged. "I didn't ask for any recommendation. I've given my word that I'll see her through this mess. England's as good a starting place for her as for me, I guess." He had a quick enmity for this woman — dislike for his inability to tell her the truth.

"Then you're completely mad, of course." She pressed a button, dismissing the subject. The maid took her instructions, dark eyes curious as she watched MacFarlane covertly.

Mrs. Whitaker opened the door to the breakfast room. Her husband was already there, wearing the rest of the gray suit — a Tattersall waistcoat. He stood splay-legged, warming himself in front of the fire.

The woman's voice was tired. "I've got to get some other clothes on. Try to stay away from one another's throats!" She shut the door on them.

MacFarlane took a seat by the window. Sarah Whitaker's raillery disturbed him. He'd been a fool ever to mention England to her. People like the Whitakers always knew someone in authority at the Home Office. As a Canadian citizen he could not be barred from the country. But Pia . . . for all he knew, the French police had a file on her.

Whitaker had been staring at the closed door. He spoke hurriedly, digging his hands deep in his pockets. "I'm not going to mince matters, MacFarlane. Ever since the day we met you, you've been the cause of trouble between my wife and me. You know only too well what I mean. Now

I want you out of this country as fast as you can go. How much will you take?"

MacFarlane sat up straight. He shook his head. "You've got it wrong, George." Shamed by the man's distress, he tried to express himself without malice. "You heard what I told Sarah — I want five hundred dollars. I meant it." For the first time he realized Whitaker's dependence on his wife. He spoke quietly. "God knows it isn't for me to tell you how to handle Sarah — but I know what I'd do with her in your place."

The ruddy eager face was somehow dignified. "What *would* you do?"

"Get rid of her!" He turned away from the shocked face.

The door opened on a maid carrying a breakfast tray. Sarah Whitaker followed. MacFarlane helped himself mechanically from steaming platters of food. The crackling fire — bright silverware — the ordered certainty of the whole procedure — all were suddenly oppressive. In a few minutes, they'd be baying down the track of a man who'd never be taken alive.

"I don't know if either of you realize just how dangerous Anstey is," he said slowly. "As far as I know he's got no weapon. But don't take it for granted. There's another thing I want understood. When I leave here, that's it! I'm not a principal in this business and I'm not a witness."

Whitaker set his cup down. "You'll have to talk to Leiclier yourself about that. I've gone as far as I can. He's the Public Prosecutor in charge of the case."

Mrs. Whitaker wore a high-necked dress of Lovat green. She was playing with the gold chain around her neck, her smile a careful production of sporting interest. "I think we ought to see the man caught — personally I wouldn't dream of missing any of the excitement."

MacFarlane nodded. It was no more than he expected. "My contract's to return everything you had stolen. No more, no less. You can have the kill on your own. I'll want a car, George, to take me into Cannes."

She was still smiling. "Then we'll all go together. Maybe your friend will need help." She shrugged. "It may take time separating her things from Anstey's."

MacFarlane's face was sober. She'd never had a charitable thought in her life. When the time came to explode her vanity, he'd do it gladly. "Whatever you like," he said indifferently. It no longer mattered whether they knew where Pia was. He got up, outstretched hand giving them the direction. "There's a house through the woods — do you know who lives there?"

The razor had left Whitaker's face with a high sheen. He worried his chin, thinking. "Some people called Crane — why?"

"Do you know them?" asked MacFarlane.

"I know their name," Whitaker said shortly. "Is that where you left her?" he asked suddenly.

"I've got to use the phone — can you get their number?"

Sarah Whitaker had the directory open. She dialed.

"Mrs. Crane — this is Sarah Whitaker! Somebody here would like to talk to you." Mouth derisive, she held the instrument to MacFarlane.

He spoke nervously. "You don't know me, Mrs. Crane, but my name's Neil MacFarlane. I'd like to speak to your husband. It's pretty urgent."

The accent was English, the tone uncertain. "I'm afraid

you can't at the moment. We've had a loose horse in the ground. Philip's just stabling it. Is there anything I could do?"

He bent, turning his face from the watching pair. "There's a woman in the car in your garage, Mrs. Crane. She's probably too scared to come out. There's no time to explain but she's been through a lot in the last couple of days. Would you bring her to the phone, please. The name is MacFarlane. Neil MacFarlane!" He wiped his mouth.

The woman's voice was frankly incredulous. "I think you must have the wrong house. I just put the car away. I had to go out to head off the horse. There's absolutely nobody here but ourselves."

He had cradled the phone before the words came, "I see. Thanks very much, Mrs. Crane." He stared, fascinated at Whitaker's Tattersall vest. He turned to the woman, shaking his head. "She's gone. Where *could* she go?"

Whitaker moved from the table impatiently. His face was skeptical. "I've been waiting for something like this." He was blocking the way to the door. "And I suppose our property's gone with her — is that the story?"

His wife hurried past, pulling MacFarlane round at the window. "How far is it from where you left Anstey to the Cranes' house?"

He looked at her blankly — remembering the gun that Pia still had — her voice as they parted. "Four or five miles. Maybe not as much. It was dark."

Her eyes were hard. "Then that's where you'll find her — with him!"

He pulled his arm free. "Get George out of my way before he gets hurt."

She stopped him from going. "Don't be a fool, Neil. Listen to me — I'm a woman. I don't know anything that may have happened between the two of you but this much is certain. She's gone back to this man because she wanted to."

Whitaker braced himself purposefully against the door. He was breathing quickly. "Give me those letters, Sarah. He's staying here till the police arrive."

MacFarlane slipped round the woman. One knee hefted the table. Its hard edge caught Whitaker's legs. Then Mac-Farlane had him by the throat, lifting him till he was standing tiptoed.

"You're going to keep your bargain," MacFarlane said savagely. "Your property's safe enough — that's all you have to worry about." He swung round on the woman. "I'm not waiting for the police, Sarah. I want a gun — a car — and some of your guards. George is going to give them the right instructions."

Whitaker knelt on the floor, looking uncertainly as his wife lit a cigarette. She moved through the debris, righting the table — picking up scattered plates. She rang the bell almost too casually. "And what do you suppose you'll do — 'shoot it out'?" Her sarcasm faded. "She's made a fool of you from the start, Neil. You're too conceited to see it."

He stopped, hand on the door handle, as the cars drove up outside. He ran to the window. Two vehicles had stopped in front of the house. Men dressed in civilian clothing were climbing from the black Citroën. The rear door of the police wagon opened. The uniformed gendarmes who jumped out all carried submachines.

Three men waited in the hall — two of them a deferential step behind the other. The main door stood open.

In the driveway beyond, a dozen gendarmes milled about, the early sun glinting on their steel helmets. A radio operator was adjusting headphones in the cab of the police wagon.

The tallest of the waiting men crossed the hall, carrying his black felt hat like a chalice. *"Bonjour,* M. Whitaker!" His broad-striped suit accentuated the length of an ungainly body bent at the shoulders. He had close-set eyes and an enormous nose that quested as he saw MacFarlane.

Whitaker opened the door to the study. The Procureur followed him in, leaving his escort outside. They sat in a tight circle. Whitaker's French was accented but voluble. Leiclier listened, eyes snapping from person to person finishing always in an open appraisal of MacFarlane. When Whitaker was done, the Procureur placed his hat carefully at his feet. He spoke in good English.

"Mr. Whitaker informs me that there has been some confusion, monsieur!" MacFarlane stared guardedly. The two men's conversation had been beyond him. Leiclier ran thumb and forefinger the length of his nose. "A complaint was lodged against you for theft. M. Whitaker now withdraws it. You understand this?"

MacFarlane was watching the man's expression carefully.

"He's withdrawing *two* complaints, isn't he?"

"Two complaints — precisely." The top half of the Procureur's body swung toward Whitaker. "There will be the formality of a signature." He came back to MacFarlane, speaking mildly. "Two complaints — only one of which concerns you. The details are scarcely clear in my mind — but as I believe, you have been held prisoner since the time of the robbery?" He waited for the answer, his attitude that of a man who prays.

MacFarlane waited till Leiclier's eyes opened before speaking.

"That's right. We were both held. In an abandoned farm by the reservoir. Anstey went into Grasse last night. That's when we managed to get free. We left the *cabanon* a couple of hours ago. As far as I know, Anstey's still there. We heard all the broadcasts — you were looking for three of us. He's got no reason to think we'd go to the police."

Leiclier was noncommittal. "It is possible. Are you able to provide a description of this man? You will appreciate that we shall need any information you have."

MacFarlane concentrated. "His hair's dyed black — he's wearing a pair of thick-framed spectacles. He's got a British passport in the name of William Spicer. I can't guarantee he's not armed — but his right hand's out of action."

Leiclier stopped him. The official went to the door — spoke to one of his escort. He took his place again, looking the length of his nose. "Very interesting. You will show me where this *cabanon* lies on the map. So you came here as soon as you were free. And Mlle. de Tellier?"

MacFarlane's voice faltered. "She couldn't walk any farther. I left her at a house a few miles away — belonging to some English people. We phoned a little while ago. She isn't there."

Mrs. Whitaker bent forward, her voice indulgent. "Isn't it quite obvious where she's gone, M. Leiclier? Back to her lover — where else?"

MacFarlane left his chair suddenly. He stood over the Procureur, holding out shaking bandaged wrists. "Neither of us committed any crime. I'm not a thief and this isn't your jail!" Leiclier had not moved. His nose pointed, sallow

130

lids sealing his eyes. MacFarlane controlled himself. "While you're asking me questions, a woman's life is in danger."

Sarah Whitaker was hauling at the back of his coat.

"Sit down, Neil! Nobody thinks you're a thief. The procureur has already told you that the complaints have been withdrawn. Everyone here is trying to help you — that's all."

He sat down — answering her was useless. He gripped the sides of his chair, measuring his words. "I'm sorry, M. Leiclier."

Leiclier stretched unhurriedly. "Your lack of courtesy is perhaps pardonable, Monsieur MacFarlane. I assume that you have no experience of police methods in our country. We are no longer concerned with your innocence — we seek now to establish the guilt of another. This requires consideration of fact. The management of your hotel in Cannes reports that you referred to Anstey as an old friend. Is this correct?"

"I'd known him a couple of hours when I said that!" answered MacFarlane. He had the idea that this man cared less for apparent facts than he suggested.

Leiclier's lower lip protruded, covering the upper part of his mouth. He nodded. "There is a history of association between this man and Mlle. de Tellier — you are possibly aware of this?"

MacFarlane chose his words. The whole truth would have been so much easier. "As far as Anstey was concerned, I was as good as dead. He talked and I listened. There's a lot I know. That she's been in jail, for instance. Years ago in Spain. I know that they were married once." Thought of the signed statements in Sarah Whitaker's bag gave him assurance. "What's it matter — there's no complaint against either of us. You've told me that yourself."

Leiclier's tone might have been either acceptance or sarcasm. His smile showed teeth capped at the gums.

"You speak of danger to this woman. I would point out two further possibilities — each more valid in my opinion. Mlle. de Tellier may still be in hiding. In hiding from you — from Anstey — from me. Or she has returned to Anstey willingly. To ascertain which we must first go to the *cabanon*."

He cranked himself from his chair and led the way out to the waiting vehicles. When he had spoken to the radio operator he walked over to the station wagon, his overcoat slung like a cloak about his shoulders. "It is perhaps better that Monsier MacFarlane accompanies me in my car as a guide." The smile was that of a ventriloquist's doll. He bowed in the Whitakers' direction. "I prefer that the rest of you stay here. There may be danger."

Sarah Whitaker buttoned her suede coat and opened the door of the station wagon. "That's nonsense. I remember what that brute did to me! If anybody has the right to see what happens, it's us." She looked at MacFarlane, her championship open. "Mr. MacFarlane can come with us. If there *is* danger, you'll tell us."

Whitaker's silence seemed to decide the Procureur. He hitched up the square-shouldered overcoat, holding the lapels together with one hand. "Very well, madame. Nevertheless you will instruct your chauffeur to keep a reasonable distance behind my car. Say thirty meters, at least." He settled the black hat firmly on his head and clambered into the rear of the Citroën. He sat slumped between two of the escort, his hand barely visible as it came up in signal. The caravan moved off.

MacFarlane sat at the back with Sarah Whitaker, shifting away from her deliberately. Whitaker was in front, a soft tweed hat jammed down over his ears. In uniform the chauffeur was devoid of personality — a man driving a car, no more. Maids were leaning from the windows of the house. The kenneled dogs set up a clamor as the cars rounded the bend.

They were past the lodge gates, on the drying highway, when the squad of helmeted motorcycle police overtook them. Leiclier craned from his door, issuing precise unhurried orders. Flanked by the motorcycles, the three vehicles accelerated to speed till they turned off on the road to the reservoir.

Sarah Whitaker had snuggled deep in her coat collar. Indifferent to his first rebuff, she sat so that her shoulder touched MacFarlane's. She stared composedly into the driving mirror, meeting her husband's eye with a faint smile.

MacFarlane looked covertly at the well-cared-for hand clutching the skin bag on her lap. Twice she had opened the bag in search of a lipstick — allowing a glimpse of the sheaf of letters inside. The shock of Pia's disappearance had driven all thought of the money from his mind. He came back to it with misgiving. Whitaker must have mentioned restitution to the Procureur yet not once had the official touched on the subject. He'd sat there — a bony receptacle for information, volunteering nothing. Memory of the man's self-containment bothered MacFarlane. The hidden money must be retrieved unseen.

Sooner or later, Leiclier had to know the truth. Maybe in

France recovery of a registered package wasn't as simple as it appeared. It was addressed to Anstey — sent by him. Even with the receipt it was possible that the Whitakers would need Leiclier's assistance.

He readied himself for the Procureur's skepticism. Things would be easier once the statements the Whitakers had signed were back in his posession.

The forest, battered and torn by the tempest, was drying in the sunlight. Wheels spun in the glutinous mud patching the surface of the road. At the bottom of the hill, the cars ahead stopped.

Leiclier climbed from the Citroën. He sniffed the air, cracking his finger joints. After a while he went across to inspect the lock on the gate to the reservoir. A man broke it open under his orders. Gendarmes piled from the police wagon, leaving only the radio operator at his controls. An aide lined the men up beyond the gate. Hat squarely on his head, Leiclier strode across to the station wagon. He pushed the top half of his body through the open window. He spoke to MacFarlane.

"There is no *cabanon* marked on our maps, monsieur. It will be necessary for you to indicate its position."

MacFarlane's hand was already on the door handle. Leiclier's gesture stopped the others from following. He called over one of his escort. The man carried a submachine gun. "You will stay in your car," Leiclier told them. "With the Inspector there is no danger."

He followed MacFarlane down the road bordering the reservoir. Fifty yards on, they climbed up to the rocky bluff, sliding in the wet clay. MacFarlane pointed. A quarter mile away, squat tortured olive trees marked the position of the house. The flat rock Anstey used as lookout point was bare in the sunshine.

"There it is! The clearing is a hundred and fifty yards across, maybe. A little less lengthways. The door and windows face the reservoir. You've got cover all the way round."

They climbed down to the road. Coat swinging, the Procureur walked the length of the drawn-up line. He gave his orders quickly, dividing the police into three main groups — five men in each. The squads separated, moving up toward the shack. The center column stayed twenty yards in the rear. Those men who remained closed about Leiclier. He removed his hat and coat, made a neat pile of them at the base of a tree. He checked the mechanism of his heavy automatic.

"*Allons-y*," he said quietly. His party disappeared into the culvert.

MacFarlane stood where he had been left, facing the concrete wall. Leaves and torn branches floated on the surface of the muddied water. Beyond its stretch, the wooded slopes lost color and form till they vanished in the growing haze.

He took a few casual steps along the wall. Twenty feet away the radio operator was busy at his controls, head bent. His voice came sharp and clear as he repeated his instructions. Police wagon and Citroën hid MacFarlane from view of the Whitaker's car. He crossed the road unhurriedly — once on the slope he started to run. Five hundred yards up, he slowed. Dense broom and bramble tore at his clothes. He trotted round the edge of the bush. The first strand of spruce was in front of him.

Stones clattered in the culvert above, the sound growing

fainter as the Procureur's party gained height. MacFarlane struck into the trees. Sun streamed through the branches dappling the ground in confused pattern. Suddenly he halted — scanning each tree — the patches of shadow — expecting Anstey to walk into the open. And because he thought of Anstey he thought of Pia. He had accepted Leiclier's suggestion gladly — imagining her flight from the garage. Frightened perhaps by the noise of a loose horse. Hers would be the heart-banging run of a terrified animal — no thought but for a new hiding place. There was barely time for her to have returned to the *cabanon*. And no sane reason.

He cupped his hands, calling her name softly. A startled bird flew up, chattering alarm. He walked on. Icy water still gushed over the cobbled bed of the gulley. He lowered himself into it and splashed up. Broken vines and wire trailed from the bank above. He straddled the culvert, lifting his head warily. The terraced earth steamed in the hot sun. At the end of the clearing, a couple of gendarmes slipped into shelter behind the house. As he watched, others took cover behind the gapped walls. He found fresh foothold, taking a firm grip on the wire dangling over his head.

Leiclier's group stood behind the ruined sheep pen. The *cabanon* door was wide open. One of the plainclothes men pulled a stone from the wall, pushing the barrel of his weapon into the embrasure. The faint breeze carried Leiclier's summation to an echo in the trees beyond.

"Anstey! Police!"

There was no answer. Leiclier chopped his arm down. The plainclothes man rose — the top half of his body well clear of the wall. He described a figure of eight with the muzzle of the machine gun, the weapon jumping in his grip. Shots spattered the front of the shack sending chipped rock flying.

Suddenly the man zigzagged from cover. He stood with his back pressed against the front wall of the house. Another burst of fire kicked mud in front of the door. Then the clearing was alive with running figures — Leiclier in the vanguard.

The Procureur came from the house, rubbing his nose thoughtfully. He stood in the doorway for a moment then swung round pointing at the heights at the back of the house. Three files of police converged toward them.

Pulling himself up, MacFarlane ran to the sheep pen. Hidden in the windowless shelter, he watched the last gendarme vanish into the trees. Anstey's scooter had been wheeled out and propped against the *cabanon* wall. Somthing lighter than the earth floor drew MacFarlane's attention. He carried the bloody rag to the door. The stains were bright and uncoagulated. His first thought was for the money. He bent, tearing at the stones that sealed his cache. The package was dry and intact.

He stuffed the banded bills into his pockets, his shirtfront, and regained the shelter. Anstey'd been back — but for what . . . MacFarlane tried following the Englishman's reasoning. Once Anstey decided that he'd been doublecrossed his return was logical. Never would he believe that MacFarlane would go to the police. Alone, possibly — with Pia, at no time. The *cabanon* was provisioned — had been chosen with care. Anstey'd watch it from somewhere till he was sure it was still safe. He could sit there another three months till he felt no danger.

MacFarlane searched the musty interior. Feeling along the beam covered with countless bird droppings — the uneven blocks that made the wall. There was no further sign of the Englishman.

The way down was reckless. MacFarlane was still running wildly when he saw the waiting group on the road below. Bates; Whitaker; the Inspector who had been left as escort.

Whitaker was straining up into the sun, his voice high with excitement. "What was the shooting — have they got him?"

MacFarlane looked down, holding the front of his shirt together. "There's nobody there. The place is empty. They've gone up into the woods behind." He ran past them, hurrying to the parked vehicles.

Sarah Whitaker had moved to the front of the station wagon. He got in beside her. She watched, narrow-eyed, as he piled the money on the seat between them.

"Count it," he said. "I've kept five hundred dollars. *You* can account for them." He stretched out a hand. "Give me the letters."

She made no move to take the money. She opened her bag slowly, her smile accentuating the bitterness in her voice.

"The letters, of course." She gave them to him.

The five envelopes made a reassuring wad on his hip.

"You were wrong, Sarah. She didn't come back." He climbed over the rear seat, stuffing the bundles of cash into the glove compartment.

Both of them turned at the noise from the slope above. Men were running down through the trees — Leiclier in the lead, leaning into his turns like a skier. MacFarlane clambered into the front of the car, speaking hurriedly. The police were coming up the road toward them.

"There's a receipt for a registered package, stuck under a chair in your guards' room. Ask Leiclier about it. The jewelry's in the package."

She was looking through the glass at the advancing men.

"This means you're really going, does it?"

The moment had been a long time coming. "With luck, I'll never see you again!" He opened the door — walked a dozen yards to meet Leiclier.

The Procureur's yellow cheeks worked like bellows. His tie was askew — the bottom halves of his trousers pasted with mud. He hung on the side of the car, speaking with difficulty.

"Come with me, monsieur!"

They made their way up to the clearing — through olive trees splashed with pale gold light — into the knot of waiting police. Pia lay on her side, her head supported by a bundled coat. A second coat had been spread across her legs. MacFarlane went down on his knees. Her eyes were shut, her face smeared by the dirt where she had fallen. He lifted her limp hand gently.

Leiclier's long legs blotted out the sunlight. He bent down, exposing the padded dressing high on the woman's breast. He covered her again. "This is Mlle. de Tellier?"

MacFarlane nodded. A pulse beat faint but regular in her throat. He climbed up, wiping his hands on the sides of his trousers.

"Anstey?"

Leiclier's head moved in assent. MacFarlane spoke as if

explaining a point of great moment, completely lost on the other.

"She couldn't help it. She came back because she couldn't help it!"

Leiclier coughed. "I've seen many wounds. Two inches to the right, as they say." He shrugged. "She will live."

A dozen men trotted up the hillside, spreading into the dense tangled forest. Four gendarmes carried Pia's wrapped body down. MacFarlane followed, dimly aware that Leiclier's hand held him steady.

Whitaker and Bates were still on the road. A few feet behind them their escort sat on the reservoir wall, sunning himself. As the small procession neared, Sarah Whitaker ran toward it, ashen-faced and stumbling.

Leiclier spread his arms, barring her way. "You will go back to your car, madame!" He walked to the Citroën, gaunt and thoughtful. Lifted with care, Pia was installed on the back seat. Two plainclothes officers took their places in front.

Leiclier crossed the road, carrying a small bottle. "You would do well to drink, Monsieur MacFarlane. It is Martinique rum."

MacFarlane tilted the bottle. A knot of warmth grew in his stomach. Suddenly he leaned against a tree, sweating. His mouth was acid with vomit. Sound of the radio operator's voice seemed to come from a great distance. He focused on Leiclier with difficulty.

The Procureur spoke patiently. "I have radioed to the hospital in Draguignan. I suggest that you accompany Mlle. de Tellier in my car."

The driver of the Citroën was waiting, motor running,

140

head turned toward the two men. MacFarlane shook himself out of the daze. He stared up beyond the trees where the flat rock shimmered in the sunlight.

"I'm staying. Anstey's somewhere up there!"

Leiclier bunched his fingers — spread them — looking into his palm with distaste. "It is extremely unlikely. The area has been searched."

MacFarlane shook his head stubbornly. The potent rum had deadened the sickness in his stomach, leaving him strong and perceptive.

"I found a rag up in the sheep pen — a quarter hour ago. It's got his blood on it. Fresh blood."

Leiclier's neck grew longer. "I left you here — what business had you to leave?"

MacFarlane told him of the money, jerking his head at the station wagon. "She's got it."

Leiclier's voice was very quiet. "I find you obstinate, monsieur. And lacking in judgment." His eyes never left MacFarlane's face. "I have seen the bandage!" He signaled the driver of the Citroën. The car moved off.

The last of the search party dropped down to the road. One man was wheeling Anstey's motor scooter. MacFarlane leaned against the tree, watching the gendarmes reassemble. The police wagon now faced east. Ahead, the curving road skirted the water. At its end the building that housed the dam controls gleamed white against a backdrop of dark green plush. Beyond that, the *maquis* stretched, an almost unbroken thicket to the Italian frontier. Instinct told him that Anstey was staked out in the vicinity, triumphant as he watched the hunt wheel on a false scent. Yet even this countryside was no permanent refuge. He'd have to move at night, avoiding the highways and populated areas. Every light in the darkness a danger — each sheepherder's fold a possible trap. Above all, the Englishman needed time. What better place to gain it than in a hiding place already searched.

The men were clambering into the police wagon. One gendarme waited in the road. He carried a submachine gun, a field radio strapped to his back. Leiclier was last up the steps. The wagon started toward the dam. MacFarlane ran after it, his shout desperate. Wheels locked — the vehicle skidded to the verge. Leiclier leaned from the open door as MacFarlane put a foot on the bottom step. The Canadian's voice was high-pitched.

"Are you all out of your minds! Can't you see what's happening — he's sitting there laughing at you!"

The gendarmes inside turned curious heads as he tried to force his way past Leiclier. The official's spare hands held unsuspected strength. He heaved MacFarlane out of the wagon.

"You will go to the Whitaker car. This time I shall ensure that you stay there."

The solitary cop on the road came running, hampered by his equipment. Leiclier's instructions were curt. The gendarmes caught MacFarlane's sleeve, twisting it in a knot.

"*Allons,* monsieur!"

Gears jarred. The wagon took the bend at high speed. MacFarlane started in the direction of the Whitaker car. They walked a few yards in this manner. Troubled by the need to hold both gun and MacFarlane, the gendarme relaxed his grip. In that instant, MacFarlane's leg anchored the other's ankles. His full weight caught the man's shoulders from behind — sending him sprawling in the dirt.

MacFarlane jumped the bank, thrashing up through clawing bramble. He kept running, leaving the gendarme's shouted fury far behind him. Here was the twilight of tall ancient pines — a hush that heightened the snap of each stick trodden underfoot. For a moment he stopped, winded and suspicious. Noise of the pursuit came from his right. Lower and down where the last scrub bush besieged the forest. Stones clattered into the culvert as he listened. He walked on. The man's first reaction would be to recapture MacFarlane himself. If he radioed Leiclier, so much the better.

The trees here were sparser. Thick-boled survivors of fire and the exigencies of woodsmen. The logger's shingle spiked one, high over MacFarlane's head. The red-daubed arrow pointed the way. Scarred earth carried the marks of a caterpillar tractor. He walked in the tracks, avoiding the rustle of stick and brush. The trail finished in a churned circle of mud and wood chippings. He lifted the edge of a staked-down tarpaulin. Steel wedges, a rusting chain and crescent saw, a heavy-headed axe. The words *Electricité de France* were branded deep in the handle.

The dump marked the start of a young plantation. Saplings sprang from the ground at chest level. He pulled himself up the banked earth, using the whipping branches as handholds. A patch of sun brightened the space ahead. Two spruce lay where they had been felled. He crawled through boughs sticky with spiderwebs. Loggers had cleared the patch marking the sudden drop. He was standing on a rocky steep, black with time and weather. Fifty feet below was the grove of olive trees. The abandoned *cabanon*, innocent in the noonday warmth. One felled trunk made a natural barrier to the granite cliff. He squirmed into the thick needles, resting his arms on the stone.

He had no plan beyond finding Anstey — no doubt that he would do so. He lay for a while watching the scene below. The clump where Pia had been found. He accepted the nature of his need for her now without embellishment, remembering her behavior with growing understanding. It didn't matter whether she'd gone back to Anstey blindly or hopefully. She'd been shot out of cold expedience. It wasn't enough that she'd live. When the time came he had to bring reason to her living.

The rocky bluff controlled house — clearing — lower forest as far as the dam. It topped the crests of the pine belt behind the *cabanon* by twenty feet. MacFarlane's tongue was dry and nervous. What he saw, maybe the Englishman saw as well. Thought of Anstey seeing yet unobserved was disquieting. MacFarlane wriggled deeper into his hide-out, turning to face the noise from the bottom of the clearing. The gendarme's head and shoulders emerged slowly from the culvert. He hauled himself up, beating at the wire that snagged his clothing. He trotted up toward the house, the machine gun in his hands. The man was hidden now in the angle of sheep pen and *cabanon*. The banging door betrayed his position. He came out of the clump of olive trees, walking slowly. Fifty yards of rough turf separated him from the forest edge. He started up the grassy slope.

Even as the man took his first step, MacFarlane saw the movement in the branches. It was high over the gendarme's head. A shaft of dirty white in the green of pinetop. A bandaged hand.

The shout died in MacFarlane's throat. A sudden cry would no more than turn the man's head — might well trip the trigger of Anstey's gun. He pressed his cheek against the warm rock, concentrating on the blur in the treetop. He was no longer afraid — but impatient for the end.

The officer returned to stand blinking in the sunlight. He was near enough for MacFarlane to see his lips work as he spoke into his field set. His way down to the clearing was hurried. He lowered himself into the watercourse in a confusion of dislodged stones. Minutes later, he was standing by the reservoir wall. A mile away, the police wagon was coming fast toward him. It halted and he climbed in the back. The Whitaker car wheeled in behind. Sound of both motors grew faint as they mounted to the highway.

A praying mantis, green and grotesque, crawled slowly across MacFarlane's still hand. The faintest breeze blew from the east, rustling the foliage that surrounded him. Nothing moved in the tree that hid Anstey — the blob of bandage had disappeared.

MacFarlane took his weight on his forearms, inching back from the edge of the drop. A sense of detachment left him beyond anger for Leiclier's stupidity. Since the first glimpse of the Englishman, MacFarlane had accepted that the issue lay between them alone. As long as he kept watch, Anstey would not escape him.

The hours wore on. Thirst troubled MacFarlane more than hunger. That and the need for a cigarette. He stayed where he was, his eyes rarely leaving the spot where the spread of an oak invaded the pinetops. Anstey's nest was a dozen yards to the left.

The last of the sun had gone — dusk climbing like a curtain pulled across the sky. The forest and clearing were

145

quiet. Occasionally a car hooted high on the Draguignan highway.

A twig snapped sharply. MacFarlane lay flat, holding his breath, the better to hear. He sensed rather than saw Anstey's first movement. The Englishman stood at the edge of the pines. His right hand was thrust into his jacket. He waited at the top of the grass slope, listening.

Suddenly he jogged down to disappear round the front of the *cabanon*. MacFarlane had dragged himself free of the fallen spruce. He was upright, staring into the twilight — ready to follow the first sound that would mean Anstey's flight. The Englishman reappeared. A blanket was thrown over his shoulder. A second cover wrapped the bundle he carried. He went back into the trees.

The sound of the climb to his refuge was distinct. The branches creaked under his weight then all was quiet again. MacFarlane had waited — tense and ready to stalk. Uncertain whether the coming of night signaled flight for the Englishman. The initiative was Anstey's. With food and covering he could sit there indefinitely or break for the *maquis* and frontier forty miles away. His tree was his stronghold. Somehow he had to be gotten out of there. Lured, coaxed or startled.

It was dark now, the shape of the *cabanon* below a mere glimmer. In the somber forest, a man with a gun held small advantage. Anstey would see no better than he could. And there was this in his favor. He knew where the Englishman was.

As quietly as he could, MacFarlane lowered himself down through the saplings. The edge of the tarpaulin caught him above the ankles. He burrowed beneath, finding the

146

heavy axe. He climbed back to his outpost. The contour of the oak tree showed round against the sharpness of the pines. He moved down, keeping his face toward it. After a while the rockface narrowed, leaving an easy drop to the grass below. As his heels dug the earth, he started running.

Yards from the verge of the trees, he went down on his belly, pushing the axe in front of him. Ears caught the rustle of branches to his left. He was no more than thirty feet from Anstey, screened by the spreading oak. He crouched in the shelter of a massive root.

"Throw your gun down, Anstey!"

He strained into the darkness, gripping the axe shaft to stop the shake in his hands. The boughs creaked then rested.

"Throw your gun down, Anstey, or I'll chop you out of there."

Something thudded to the ground. He moved as if walking toward it. Anstey fired twice — bullets plowing the earth.

Between oak and Anstey, a pine leaned out of perpendicular. For a moment, MacFarlane stood unprotected, swinging the axe into the soft wood. Three bites of the blade notched the tree ready for felling. He ran behind its trunk. The head of the axe rang with the force of his blows. The shaft split in his hands. Dropping the axe, he leaned his weight on the toppling trunk. The pine crashed into Anstey's eyrie, splintering branches as it tore its way to the ground.

There were two more shots. Then the heavy cans of provisions hurtled toward the oak where MacFarlane lay. He heard the noise of Anstey's descent. Legs pumping, Mac-Farlane followed. He no longer saw where he ran, hearing his own croaked breathing with despair. Suddenly the whole forest was lighted. Fifty yards ahead, Anstey stopped in the glare of searchlights. No more than a second, he waited. Then lifting his gun, he fired into his temple. His legs buckled under him. He pitched slowly forward.

MacFarlane had stopped to a walk. He stood looking down at Anstey. The hole in the near side of the Englishman's head was almost clinical in its neatness. The weapon that had made it lay a few feet away in the bracken. He picked it up, checking the empty magazine automatically. He let it fall and went to meet the ring of advancing gendarmes. Hands helped him up the hill to the highway.

The line of covered trucks stretched for a hundred yards. Mounted searchlights still stabbed the forest. He recognized Leiclier's scarecrow silhouette and turned away. A ditch held water — he sat there washing his hands and face. When he'd done, he walked slowly up the road away from the lights and the shouted confusion. A car moved after him. Leiclier leaned from the window, his voice kindly.

"It is a long way to walk to Draguignan."

MacFarlane nodded. "A long way." He climbed into the police car, the pressure on his arm a reassuring thing.

>>> If you've enjoyed this book and would like to discover more great vintage crime and thriller titles, as well as the most exciting crime and thriller authors writing today, visit: >>>

The Murder Room
Where Criminal Minds Meet

themurderroom.com

www.ingramcontent.com/pod-product-compliance
Ingram Content Group UK Ltd.
Pitfield, Milton Keynes, MK11 3LW, UK
UKHW040436280225
455666UK00003B/119